Fun Bedtime Stories for Kids Ages 4-8

ADVENTUROUS SHORT STORIES PACKED WITH LIFE LESSONS
DESIGNED TO BUILD CHARACTER AND STIMULATE YOUNG,
INQUISITIVE MINDS AS THEY HAPPILY DRIFT OFF TO SLEEP

Penelope Arnoll-Davis

Contents

Introduction VII

1. Noah and Millie's Bedtime Rituals 1
    Sleepyheads
    The Sleepover Mystery
    The Moonlit Lullaby
    The Dream Catchers
    Onto the Next Adventure...

2. Backyard Playtime Adventures 17
    The Adventure Box
    The Painting Pals
    The Cardboard Kingdom
    The Imagination Circus
    Onto the Next Adventure...

3. Friendship and Kindness 33
    The Cookie Surprise
    The Playground Buddies
    The Kindness Club
    The Forgiving Dandelion
    Onto the Next Adventure...

4. Brave Escapades in the Neighborhood 49
    The Mysterious Missing Key

The Daring Rescue Operation

The Great Garden Challenge

The Friendly Neighborhood Cleanup

Onto the Next Adventure...

5. Family and Love   63

The Surprise Party

The Family Talent Show

The Camping Adventure

The Family Recipe

Onto the Next Adventure...

Make a Difference with Your Review   79

Make a Difference with Your Review

6. Nature Expedition   81

The Secret Trail

The Animal Whispers

Nature's Symphony

Farewell, National Park

Onto the Next Adventure...

7. The Power of Confidence and Acceptance   95

The Bold Performer

The Brave Explorers

The Unique Puzzle Piece

The Confident Leader

Onto the Next Adventure...

8. Noah and Millie's Quest for Wonder   109

The Space Explorers

The Amazing Museum

The Time Travelers

Onto the Next Adventure...

9. The Power of Gratitude   121
    The Kindness Jars
    A Blessing in Disguise
    The Appreciation Picnic
    Onto the Next Adventure...

10. The Fearless Ventures   133
    Fearless Millie
    The Rescue Mission
    I Am Brave!
    Onto the Next Adventure...

Conclusion   145
    Your book review is more than words.

Introduction

Adventure Awaits!

Once upon a time, in a land of dreams,

Where imagination soared with endless streams,

Lived Noah and Millie, our young heroes bold,

Their stories to be told, tales to unfold.

Dearest Parents,

Welcome to a world of adventure and imagination!

In this delightful book of *Fun Bedtime Stories for Kids Ages 4-8*, your young one will get to embark on happy journeys alongside our beloved characters, Noah and Millie.

Children often find joy in the wonderful world of storytelling. Your child's bedtime can become a gateway to adventures, where dreams blend seamlessly with reality.

It is within these pages that your little one will be transported to the land of captivating stories that entertain and inspire. Each tale is infused with valuable life lessons, teaching the importance of compassion, kindness, courage, and the power of imagination.

So, snuggle up, turn the pages, and prepare for a world of discovery!

With each story, we hope to inspire, entertain, and leave young readers with a sense of wonder while discovering valuable life lessons. As your child happily drifts off to sleep, their mind filled with contentment, may their dreams be as adventurous as the stories they've just experienced.

With Gratitude and Warm Wishes,
Penelope Arnoll-Davis

Chapter 1

Noah and Millie's Bedtime Rituals

SLEEPYHEADS

After having a delicious dinner, Noah, aged nearly five, and his big sister Millie, aged eight, both felt wide awake. The two children had gone to the zoo with their parents that day, and even though they were already tired, they were too excited to sleep. After brushing their teeth and wearing their pajamas, they sat on their beds with smiles on their faces.

"Why are you two still up?" Mom asked when she came into their room to tuck them in. "What happened to my two sleepyheads?"

"We're just too excited, Mom!" Noah exclaimed.

"Going to the zoo was the best! Can we go there again soon?" asked Millie.

"Sure. But first, you two need to go to sleep. You have school tomorrow," Mom said with a smile.

Noah and Millie glanced at each other. Then Noah looked at Mom and said, "Can you tell us a bedtime story first?"

Mom pretended to think about it for a while, then she smiled and said, "Of course. Bedtime stories are best told before bed. Now get into bed, both of you, so that I can share a very special story with you about sleepyheads."

"But... aren't *we* the sleepyheads?" Millie asked with a giggle.

"Yes!" Mom answered cheerfully. "But we just came from the zoo today and I know you'd love to hear about the sleepyheads of the animal kingdom too. Just like you, they all get ready for bed and go to sleep in different ways."

"Really?" Millie asked with a twinkle in her eyes.

"But... how can you sleep in different ways?" wondered Noah.

"Well, as you know, there are different kinds of animals all over the world," Mom began. "Some of them are a lot like us. Orangutans use leaves and twigs to make mattresses for them to sleep on just like how you two are lying down on the mattresses of your beds.

"But then there are funny little creatures called meerkats who sleep on top of each other! They sleep in piles to keep warm and make sure that everyone is safe. Would you be able to sleep comfortably if we all slept in one pile too?"

"No!" cried the two children, giggling.

"Sometimes though, when I sleep with you, I like to hold your hand," Millie said.

"That's right! I like that too. And when we do that, we sleep just like sea otters who snooze while holding hands with each other. Such cute little sleepyheads," Mom said with a smile as she watched Noah and Millie yawn.

But before the two sleepyheads drifted off, Mom asked, "Even animals need to prepare for bed so that they will have sweet dreams. How about you, how do you two prepare for bed?"

"By following our bedtime routine," Millie said sleepily. "You said that having a bedtime routine will help us sleep soundly every night."

"First of all, our room has to be dim, but not too dark!" Noah said, yawning. "Our beds have to be comfy too. Once we're comfy, it's time for a bedtime story just like the one you're telling us now."

"You're right. Animals like to sleep in the dark too. But if you ever go into a dark cave, you might be surprised when you see that bats sleep upside-down. Or if you find a flock of flamingos, your eyes might grow wide as you see that they sleep while standing up," shared Mom with her voice growing softer by the minute.

Then Mom gently covered the children in blankets as she said, "Just like you, all the animals have their own ways of sleeping. And just like you, all the animals have their own routines too. Like you said, following your routine makes it easier for you to fall asleep and have sweet dreams."

The two sleepyheads fell asleep with smiles on their faces. Mom gave each of them a kiss and promised to continue telling them about the other sleepyheads of the animal world the next night. When Mom left, the two children slept peacefully all night.

When Noah and Millie woke up the next day, they felt energized and refreshed.

"That was the best sleep I've had in forever!" Millie said cheerfully.

"Me too. And I think it was because we followed our bedtime routine just like the animals in the zoo. Mom and Dad always told us that a good night's sleep is important. Now, I know why," Noah said.

"You're right! We feel so wonderful this morning because we slept really well last night!" Millie agreed.

Since then, Noah and Millie have always followed their bedtime routine just like all the animals they love so much.

THE SLEEPOVER MYSTERY

It was a very exciting day for Noah and Millie.

The two children were invited by one of their cousins to sleep over at her house. They had spent all morning packing their bags and thinking of activities to do at their cousin's house.

Now that they were on their way, Noah and Millie felt very excited!

"I can't wait to play games with our cousins," said Noah.

"And I can't wait to see what kind of snacks Auntie Jenn prepared for us," Millie said with a grin.

When they arrived at their cousin's house, the two children said goodbye to Mom and Dad. Then they ran inside to join their cousins who were already in the living room.

"Oh, wow!" exclaimed Millie when she saw that the living room was transformed into their sleepover space.

There was a tent in the middle and pillows were scattered all over the floor. Their cousin Tiffany walked over as soon as she saw them. She was the one who invited them and some of their other cousins to her sleepover.

The sleepover started splendidly. Noah, Millie, and all of their cousins had a lot of fun playing games, watching movies, and cooking their own dinner. When it was time to sleep, they were all very tired.

"Good night, everyone," said Noah.

"Good night," said Millie with a yawn.

And the two children lay down in their sleeping bags. But just as they were about to close their eyes, they heard a strange noise.

Tap. Tap. Thump!

"Did you hear that?" Noah asked as he sat up.

"It sounded like it came from the window," Millie said.

Tap. Tap. Thump!

Tap. Tap. Thump!

"What is that sound?" asked Jennifer, one of their cousins. She sounded scared.

"Maybe it's just the wind," suggested Jordan, Jennifer's brother.

"I've never heard the wind sound like that before," Tiffany said.

Tap. Tap. Thump!

Jennifer whimpered fearfully, so Millie walked over and sat with her. She said, "Don't be scared. We're all here together. Besides, it's just a sound."

"Millie's right. But we should try to find out what's making that sound," Noah said bravely as he stood up.

"I guess you're right," Jordan agreed as he stood up too.

"Okay. But how do we find the noise?" Tiffany wondered.

"First, we will need a flashlight. Do you have one?" asked Noah.

Tiffany nodded, then left the living room. Moments later, she came back with a small flashlight in her hand.

Noah thanked his cousin as she handed him the flashlight. He clicked it on and said, "Let's all form one long line. We'll hold each other's shoulders and look out for what could be causing the sound."

"That's a good idea," Millie said. "Noah will lead the way with the flashlight. That way, we will all be together."

Noah turned the flashlight on, and all of his cousins lined up behind him. When they were ready, they started walking together. They tiptoed across the floor while looking around.

It was very quiet in the house, and they didn't hear the sound again. Millie wondered if they would still hear the mysterious noise. The children kept walking until they reached the window next to the front door.

Tap. Tap. Thump!

Tap. Tap. Thump!

Tap. Tap. Thump!

"Th-there's the sound again," Jennifer stammered as her eyes widened.

"It's getting louder," Noah whispered.

Just then, Millie saw something moving outside. She pointed in that direction and exclaimed, "Look out there!"

The cousins all looked at what Millie was pointing at. Then they all gasped as they saw a pair of big yellow eyes looking at them. Everyone felt scared and they all started shivering. Then Noah shined his flashlight toward the window.

To their delight, they saw that the two big eyes belonged to a friendly old owl. It was perched on a branch outside.

Tap. Tap. Thump!

Tap. Tap. Thump!

As the wind blew, it moved the branch and caused the tapping sound. And when the branch moved, the owl flapped its wings so it wouldn't lose its balance.

Tap. Tap. Thump!

Tap. Tap. Thump!

"It's just an owl," Jennifer said with relief.

"An owl that's trying not to fall off the branch," Noah said with a chuckle.

"That solves the mystery!" exclaimed Millie cheerfully.

Then Noah, Millie, and their cousins went back to the living room. They all realized that facing their fears showed them how things weren't always as scary as they seemed. Since then, Noah and Millie have become much braver children.

THE MOONLIT LULLABY

Camping was always something that Noah and Millie really enjoyed. They were curious, energetic, and loved going on adventures. For the longest time, they had been begging their parents to let them go on a camping trip.

Many of their friends had shared stories about camping with their parents. Each story they heard made the two children feel even more excited about spending a night under the stars.

One summer morning, to their delight, their parents gave them some wonderful news.

"It's such a beautiful day today," said Dad while eating breakfast.

"You're right. It's the perfect day to go camping," Mom said with a smile.

"What did you just say?" Noah asked, his eyes wide.

"Are we going... camping?" Millie asked with a gasp.

"Only if you are up for it," Dad said even though he already knew the answer.

"YES!" cried the two children excitedly.

And so, Noah, Millie, and their parents got ready for their first camping trip as a family. The two children were very excited while they packed their bags. Since it was their first time, they didn't know what to take.

"We should pack clothes, toys, and... what else?" Millie wondered.

"Toothbrushes?" Noah asked with a grin.

After packing, the two children loaded their stuff in the car. Then the whole family left for the campsite.

Once there, the two children excitedly helped their parents pitch the tent. It was a challenging task, but it was a lot of fun too. When they were done, Noah and Millie felt proud of themselves.

As Mom and Dad prepared their dinner, the two children explored the campsite. They skipped around the campsite happily while chanting,

Nature, nature is all around.

Beautiful sights and sweet sounds.

The morning sunshine feels so nice,

And the cold night air feels like ice!

This was a short rhyme that their parents taught them when they were younger. They always sang it whenever they were enjoying the outdoors. To Noah and Millie, this was the perfect day for their chant.

"I can't believe we're finally on a camping trip," Millie said.

"I can't wait for the sun to set. This will be our first time to see the night sky while outside," Noah commented.

For the rest of the afternoon, Noah and Millie continued to explore. They saw so many cool things like tall trees, bushes with colorful leaves, and even a few furry creatures running around.

When Mom called them for dinner, the two children raced back to their tent. Exploring had made them very hungry and it was fun eating outside. They felt like the food that Mom prepared tasted even better when eaten in the great outdoors.

"I love these hotdogs, Mom!" Noah exclaimed.

"And this stew is the best stew you've ever cooked," commented Millie with a grin.

After they finished their meal, Dad laid a mat on the ground next to their tent. It was time for stargazing.

Noah, Millie, and their parents lay down on the mat and looked up at the sky.

"It's so beautiful," Millie said softly as she was starting to get sleepy.

"There are so many stars!" Noah exclaimed, then he yawned as he was getting a bit sleepy too.

Then the two children listened as Dad told them stories about the constellations in the sky.

"Constellations are groups of stars that form images in the sky," Dad explained.

Then he pointed to the stars that belonged to each constellation. Noah and Millie followed Dad's finger with their eyes so that they could imagine the constellations in their minds. All of the constellations were quite beautiful.

Camping was truly a treat for them as they had a magical night under the stars. They also listened to the soothing sounds of nature around them. They could hear crickets chirping, owls hooting softly, and even a soft breeze blowing through the trees. All those sounds made Noah and Millie feel very sleepy.

As the two children drifted off to sleep, Mom sang a lullaby for them.

Sleep now, dear ones under the lovely night sky.

Close your eyes and let your imaginations fly.

Sleep well, dear ones, on this peaceful night.

And go along as your dreams take flight.

While Mom sang softly, Noah and Millie smiled in their sleep. Mom's lullaby always gave them sweet dreams.

It had been an amazing day for the two children as they learned how to appreciate the beauty of the world around them and find comfort in the great outdoors.

THE DREAM CATCHERS

Have you ever tried catching a dream before?

Not everyone can catch dreams. In fact, many people don't even remember their dreams when they wake up!

But this is exactly what two little children tried doing one night before they went to sleep.

It was a worrisome night for Noah and Millie. It was raining very hard outside, and the rain even came with thunder and lightning. Thunderstorms made the two children feel scared.

"Come on, get into bed, both of you," Mom said after they finished brushing their teeth and wearing their pajamas.

The two little children did as they were told and waited for Mom and Dad to tuck them in. Even though there was a storm outside, it was quite a special night as their grandparents had come to visit. So, they also waited for Grandma and Grandpa to kiss them goodnight.

"Good night," said Mom.

"Sweet dreams," said Dad.

"Sleep tight," said Grandpa.

"And try to catch your dreams," whispered Grandma with a wink.

When everyone left, and the two children were left in the dark, Noah sat up. He looked at his sister and said, "Did Grandma whisper the same thing to you?"

Millie sat up too and nodded, "You mean about catching our dreams?"

The little boy hopped off his bed and walked over to Millie. He sat on her bed and asked, "Do you know how to do that?"

Millie shook her head, "I didn't even know that people could do that!"

Then the two children stayed quiet for a while as they thought about what their grandma had told them. Moments later, they heard a soft knock on the door.

"Come in," said Noah softly.

The door opened slowly, and Grandma's face peeked from behind it. She smiled sweetly and said, "I see that you're both up."

Noah and Millie ran to the door and pulled Grandma inside their room. Then the little girl said, "Please tell us how to catch our dreams!"

"Alright," said Grandma. "But only because you two are the best grandchildren in the world. Now, hop into bed."

The two children did as they were told, then Grandma pulled up a chair. She placed the chair in the middle of Noah and Millie's beds, then sat down. Before talking, Grandma told the children to lie back down in their beds.

"It's time to use your imagination," said Grandma. "Close your eyes, take a deep breath, and listen to my voice. Imagine yourself walking near a stream. A long stream with blue water. Do you want to swim in the stream?"

"Yes!" cried Noah and Millie.

"Wonderful! But, when you try to go near the water, you realize that you can't because there are thorny branches scattered all over the ground!"

"Oh, no!" said Millie with a furrowed brow.

"What will we do?" Noah wondered with a frown.

"What do you think you should do?" asked Grandma.

The two children opened their eyes and stared at each other. Then they both smiled.

"I think I saw a big broom leaning on one of the trees," Noah said.

"A broom? In a forest near a stream? How imaginative!" Grandma exclaimed, which made Millie giggle.

"Yes!" said Noah excitedly. "Millie and I can take turns sweeping the thorny branches away, then we can jump in the stream and swim as long as we want."

"I think that's an amazing idea," Grandma agreed. "Now, close your eyes and catch those thoughts you have. Catching your happy thoughts and keeping them with you will make it easier for you to have happy dreams when you fall asleep."

"Really?" Millie asked with wide eyes.

"Yes! Whenever you feel sad or worried, you can both use your imaginations to go on adventures together," Grandma explained. "I know that you're both feeling worried tonight because of the thunderstorm. But if you try to change those worries to happy thoughts, you will discover the hidden dreamland within this lovely bedroom of yours."

"How did you know that we felt worried?" Noah wondered.

"A grandma always knows," she said gently.

Then she kissed Noah and Millie on their foreheads. As they watched the door close behind their grandma, the two children felt more relaxed. Even though it was still raining outside, they didn't feel scared anymore.

Using their imagination to solve a problem helped them become braver, stronger, and smarter too! So, Noah and Millie drifted off to sleep with smiles on their faces, both ready to start catching happy dreams.

ONTO THE NEXT ADVENTURE...

Did you enjoy these bedtime stories?

Noah and Millie had lots of fun discovering different ways to sleep while learning important lessons along the way. They found out the importance of bedtime routines, letting go of their worries before going to bed, and even overcoming challenges. All of these helped them sleep soundly and have sweet dreams.

Now, it's time to go outside and have some adventures in the backyard with Noah and Millie!

Chapter 2

Backyard Playtime Adventures

THE ADVENTURE BOX

N oah and Millie loved playing in their backyard. To them, the backyard wasn't just a part of their home. It was a place where they made many special memories together. They enjoyed sunny days the most and today was extra special as they discovered something amazing!

"Let's play hide-and-seek, Millie!' exclaimed Noah.

Millie agreed happily and said, "I'll count. Just remember, you can only hide in places around the backyard, okay?"

Noah nodded, so Millie closed her eyes and started counting. But before she could count up to ten, she heard Noah scream!

"Millie!"

"What is it?!" cried the little girl as she opened her eyes and looked around for her brother.

She saw Noah on the other side of the backyard, right beside one of Mom's rose bushes. He was squatting on the ground, staring at something behind the bush.

Millie ran over to Noah and asked, "Are you okay?"

"M-hm," said the little boy with a nod. "But I found something cool."

Millie looked at what Noah was pointing to. Then her eyes grew wide as she saw a mysterious box on the ground. It was small, black, and it looked very old.

Millie reached over and grabbed the box. Then she placed it on the ground between her and Noah.

"What do you think it is?" wondered the little boy.

"There's only one way to find out," said Millie.

She gently lifted the lid of the box while smiling excitedly. Inside, they saw a bunch of different things like silver bells, an old toy boat, a broken little ship, and more.

"Oh... I thought there was something cool inside," muttered Noah with disappointment.

Millie felt sad that Noah was disappointed. So, she thought of a way to make the box more exciting.

She said, "What are you talking about? This is definitely cool! I think we have found an adventure box and if we both use our imagination, we can invent a pretend world of our own, using these things. For example..."

Millie took the two silver bells and said, "Let's pretend that these are the greatest and most precious treasures of the king and we just found them! They are... um... silver crystal bells that ring when special things happen!"

"Wow!" exclaimed Noah. "Do they really? That's brilliant!"

"Yes!" Millie answered. "The king lost these bells when he visited another kingdom a long time ago, and he has been looking for them ever since."

Feeling excited, the little boy rummaged through the box too. He grabbed the toy boat and said, "We need to take the treasure back to the king! Let's ride on this cool boat!"

"That's perfect!" Millie said with a giggle, and so, the two children began their adventure.

When they stood up the box toppled over, and the broken ship fell out. Suddenly, it started to grow...

With wide eyes, the two children imagined that they could see the small ship turning into a huge one! And it also had a pirate's flag on it.

"Uh-oh," said Millie. "Pirates."

"What are we going to do?!" Noah cried.

"We can't let them grab our silver bells!" Millie yelled while running.

Just then, Millie had an idea. She grabbed the box, knelt down, and rummaged through the contents. "This adventure box is filled with useful objects. We need to find something that we can use to get away from those pirates."

"How about these?" Noah asked as he picked up two wooden spoons. "We can use them as oars!"

"That's perfect!" Millie exclaimed.

"Let's hop onto our boat, Millie!" cried Noah.

The two children jumped into their imaginary boat, using the two wooden spoons as oars to paddle away.

"Faster! Faster!" Millie yelled with a giggle. "We need to get ahead of the pirate ship!"

Soon, they saw the castle of the king. It was actually their house. Once there, they jumped off their boat and ran inside.

They ran all around the house until they spotted their dad who was chopping some vegetables in the kitchen.

"Here you go, your majesty," said Noah with a bow as he handed the silver bells to Dad.

"Hey, these are my silver bells!" Dad said in surprise. "I've been looking everywhere for these. Where did you find them?"

"In a treasure chest outside," said Millie with a grin.

"Thank you," Dad said, smiling, as he took the bells from Noah. "You two are having lots of fun outside, aren't you?"

Smiling wide, the two children ran back outside. They wanted to have more fun in the backyard with their super cool adventure box. They knew they'd be discovering other exciting things!

The Painting Pals

Staying with Grandpa and Grandma was always a treat for Noah and Millie. They loved their grandparents very much. Whenever they came over, Grandma or Grandpa always thought of fun things for them to do.

"Are you ready to go?" Mom asked as she stood by the front door of their house.

"All set!" answered the two children excitedly.

Mom, Noah, and Millie hopped into the family car. They sang songs while Mom drove all the way to Grandma and Grandpa's house.

"There you are!" cried Grandma as soon as Mom parked the car in front of the house.

"Come on, come on," said Grandpa as he helped the two children get out of the car.

"See you later, Mom!" Millie said before getting out, while Noah had already run inside his grandparent's house.

After Mom left, the little girl followed her grandparents inside the house. To Millie's surprise, they went straight to the backyard. Once there, the little girl's eyes twinkled with delight. In the backyard, Grandma and Grandpa had prepared two blank canvases.

They were propped up on easels and they were huge!

Grandma used to be a painter, and she believed that the two children were amazing painters too.

"What's all this?" asked the little girl.

"These are the things your grandma and I prepared for you to do today. You've seen the canvases. Now, on the table are different types of paint that you can use. Today is going to be a messy day as you can both paint whatever you want," Grandpa explained.

"Wow!" Noah exclaimed.

"Thank you so much!" said Millie cheerfully.

Before the two children started, their grandparents gave them aprons to wear.

"We don't want your clothes to get dirty or we might get in trouble with your mom," Grandpa said with a chuckle.

"While you do that, I'll start baking your favorite cookies," said Grandma.

"Chocolate chip cookies with mini marshmallows?" Noah asked, grinning from ear to ear.

"Of course!" answered Grandma with a wink.

After putting on his apron, Noah started painting right away. He dipped his paintbrush in blue paint and started painting the outline of a car. He was so happy that he hummed while he worked.

But Millie didn't start just yet. She had many ideas of what to paint, but she didn't know how to start. The little girl took one of the paintbrushes and sat on the chair in front of her blank canvas.

"Come on, sis! Start painting!" Noah urged.

"I will. I just... don't know what to paint yet," Millie replied.

While Noah painted next to her excitedly, Millie just stared at her blank canvas. She focused on her many ideas one at a time, but she didn't know which one to pick. The little girl kept staring in front of her until she felt a hand touch her shoulder.

Millie looked up in surprise and saw Grandma smiling down at her. She asked, "Is everything okay?"

"I don't know what to paint," Millie said as she glanced at her brother.

To her surprise, he had already painted so much!

"When did you paint all that?"

"Just now," Noah answered with a grin. "I kept painting while you stared at your canvas for the longest time."

Millie also noticed the smell of cookies coming from the kitchen, so she turned to Grandma, "Are you done making the cookies?"

"Yes, they're baking in the oven," Grandma answered. "I even cleaned up the kitchen. And when I came out here, I was surprised to see that your canvas is still blank. Is everything okay?"

"I just... don't know what to paint," Millie admitted.

With a smile, Grandma said, "Painting isn't something you need to think about too much. Just let your imagination flow and let it guide your hands to create something beautiful."

Millie smiled. Then she dipped her paintbrush in a can of yellow paint and started swishing it on the canvas.

"Keep going," Grandma encouraged.

The little girl kept adding colors to her canvas. The more colorful it became, the happier she felt. Now, she knew why her Grandma loved painting so much!

When they were both finished, Grandma and Grandpa were amazed at their works of art. Noah had painted a blue and red car in the middle of a desert filled with different types of cacti.

Millie had painted a rainbow using different colors. Around her rainbow were little butterflies with sparkling wings. She'd used Grandma's glittery paint to make the wings. Both children were proud of their work, and they felt very happy after expressing themselves through art.

And the best part was, Grandma's cookies were ready when their painting was done.

THE CARDBOARD KINGDOM

Noah and Millie felt thrilled as they were about to have a super fun day ahead of them. It was Saturday morning, and they were waiting for their friends to arrive at their house. They had invited their friends over to play the whole day.

After getting dressed, the two children went to the backyard to wait. The backyard was one of their favorite places in the world.

In the backyard, their imaginations came to life, and they couldn't wait to play with their friends there too.

"Whoa!" exclaimed Noah when he saw what was in the backyard.

Right in the middle of the backyard was a pile of boxes. There were big boxes, small boxes, brown boxes, and colorful boxes. Noah and Millie thought those boxes looked familiar.

"What are these boxes doing here?" Millie wondered.

"Well, I just spent the whole week cleaning out the garage," Mom answered. "While cleaning, I ended up with all these empty boxes. I was about to throw them away when I realized that you can use them today!"

"We can use these boxes to build a castle!" said Millie excitedly.

"Or a rocket to the moon!" cried Noah while jumping up and down.

"Exactly! Your play date with your friends has come at the perfect time. I know that you love using your imaginations here in the backyard. These boxes will just make things more fun for you," Mom said.

Just then, a knock came at the front door. The two children ran to the door excitedly and opened it. Their friends came in and they all ran to the backyard to see what Mom had prepared.

"Wow! Look at all of these boxes!" said Briana, one of their friends.

"We can build a cardboard kingdom with all of these boxes!" cried Ethan, another one of their friends.

"That's exactly what I was thinking," Millie agreed.

So, the children got to work. They started stacking the boxes on top of each other to build different things. First, they built a castle with a moat. It was a very colorful castle since they used the boxes with different colors.

After building their castle, the children pretended to have a royal tournament. They played different games where the boys played against the girls. Noah, Millie, and their friends had a lot of fun competing with each other.

After their royal adventure, they toppled the castle over and used the boxes to build a huge spaceship.

"It's time to set off to Outer Space!" Noah said as he sat in the captain's seat.

Since it was Noah's idea to build the spaceship, they all agreed that he could be the captain. While his crew rode with him, the rest of the children each took a box for themselves. They had a different role to play.

Noah and his crew used their imagination to bring their spaceship to life. They zoomed through space, then landed on a planet where they met aliens. Millie and the other girls were really good at pretending to be aliens! And they used the boxes they took as their houses on their planet.

When they finished exploring the alien planet, they took their spaceship apart, and built a fort.

"We need to protect our fort from invaders!" cried Ben, another friend of theirs.

Half of the children stayed inside the fort while the other half threw pillows at the fort as they pretended to be the invaders.

By the time they brought the fort down, all of the children were giggling happily.

"It looks like you're having so much fun!" Mom exclaimed.

She walked into the backyard while carrying a tray filled with some glasses, a pitcher of milk, and a big plate of cookies.

"You're just in time, Mom! We're starving!" cried Noah.

All of the children thanked Mom for the snack. Then they sat on the grass and passed the milk and cookies around for everyone to share.

While eating, they made more plans for what they would build with the boxes. It was truly a fun-filled afternoon for Noah and Millie. They were able to work together with their friends while having fun and using their imaginations.

For the rest of the afternoon, the children built many other things. When it was time to go home, everyone was tired and happy. They all wanted to keep playing, so the two children promised to have them over again the next weekend.

"And don't worry, we'll have the boxes ready," promised Millie with a smile.

THE IMAGINATION CIRCUS

Ever since they could remember, Noah and Millie had been very interested in the circus. Even though they hadn't been to a real circus yet, the two children were fascinated with the circuses they saw on TV. They thought that clowns were funny, acrobats were amazingly flexible, and jugglers were super cool. The two children also loved seeing different animals in the circus.

"What do you think it feels like to be part of a circus?" Noah wondered one morning while he hung out with Millie in their backyard.

"I think it would be a lot of fun," Millie said with a smile. "If I joined the circus, I would be an acrobat. I would fly through the air in a beautiful costume that sparkles with shiny gems."

"If I joined the circus, I would be a lion tamer!" exclaimed Noah excitedly. "Not just lions. I would tame tigers, bears, and elephants too, and like other animal trainers, I would take good care of my animals."

Then the little boy sighed as he sat on the grass, dreaming of the Big Top and circus life. He said, "I wonder what it would feel like to be part of a circus."

"We don't have to keep wondering, you know," Millie said cheerfully.

"What do you mean?" Noah asked.

"We have a big backyard! It's big enough to house an entire circus! All we need are some decorations and our amazing imaginations," said the little girl with a twinkle in her eyes.

"Wow! You're right!" said the little boy excitedly as he stood up. "Where do we start?"

Millie grabbed her brother's arm and pulled him into the house. They looked for Mom and asked her if they could borrow her party decorations. After their mom agreed, the two children took her box of decorations and went back to the backyard.

"Let's start by decorating our circus," Millie said. "All circuses are full of colors. Our backyard is a beautiful place but it's not colorful enough."

Together, Noah and Millie hung streamers on tree branches, scattered paper lanterns on the grass, and covered the bushes with colorful table cloths. They sang songs while working, which lifted their spirits up even more. Soon, their backyard disappeared as it had become a colorful circus for the two children to play in.

"We're ready!" Millie exclaimed.

"And here come the animals!" Noah said excitedly.

Their eyes twinkled as they imagined elephants, lions, bears and tigers coming into their circus. As the animal trainer, Noah led the circus animals to their places. Instead of putting them in cages, Noah led the animals to one side of the circus.

Before the performance, Noah even fed his animals so they wouldn't be hungry while performing. Since Noah was an amazing animal trainer, all of the animals sat quietly and waited for their turn to perform.

"The jugglers have arrived too," Millie said with a smile. "And here come the clowns! They're the funniest clowns on the planet!"

"You'd better get dressed, Millie. I can see the acrobats flying through the air. They'll be here soon for you to join them, and you should be ready," suggested the little boy.

Millie giggled and nodded her head. Then she quickly went inside the house and changed into her gymnastics uniform. It didn't have the sparkling gems that she wanted, but it looked a lot like what acrobats in circuses wore. When she came back outside, she saw that all the other members of their circus had arrived.

"It's time to start!" she said happily.

As the show started, the two children had tons of fun imagining each part of their circus. Noah clapped loudly as Millie flew through the air with her acrobat friends. The little girl had watched so many videos of acrobats and trapeze artists that she knew exactly how to move like them.

When it was Noah's turn to perform with his circus animals, he lined them all up. Then he dressed the animals in colorful outfits so they would fit in perfectly with the rest of their circus. As Noah's animals performed, Millie cheered loudly for them.

Noah and Millie were each other's biggest fans. They always cheered for each other, whether they were playing or competing in real competitions.

While playing, Noah and Millie learned how to work together better. They worked together to decorate the backyard, then they both used their unique imaginations to think of fantastic ideas. It was truly a fun and special day for the two children as they brought their backyard circus to life.

Onto the Next Adventure...

Did you know that you can have tons of fun adventures in your backyard?

Noah and Millie enjoyed playing and doing other fun activities in their backyard while learning some helpful lessons too. They used their imaginations to make their days more interesting, which is something you can do too!

Now, it's time to learn more about friendship and kindness with Noah and Millie...

Chapter 3

Friendship and Kindness

THE COOKIE SURPRISE

Noah and Millie had lots of friends. They were both kind, cheerful, and friendly. They were also very thoughtful and generous. Noah and Millie were always thinking of ways to make their friends happy. Whenever they did something nice for their friends, they felt good too. So, they did not miss any chance to be kind toward others.

One morning, the two children talked about what had happened in class the day before. Their class was supposed to go on a field trip, but it had been raining so hard the past few days that their teacher decided to cancel their field trip.

"Everyone was so sad yesterday," said Millie with a sigh.

"I was sad too. I really wanted to go on the field trip," Noah said.

"But our teacher said that it wouldn't be safe for us to go. She also said that we wouldn't be able to explore the different places because of the rain," Millie explained.

Noah sighed, pulling a long face. Just like Millie and the rest of their friends, the little boy felt excited when they first heard about the field trip. They were supposed to go to a big flower park, then to an amusement park.

Then when their teacher called the field trip off, he felt disappointed too.

"Do you think there's something we can do to make everyone feel better?" Noah wondered.

"I don't know. Maybe you have some ideas?" Millie asked.

The two children were quiet for a while as they tried to think of what could make their friends feel better. All of a sudden, they both jumped up and grinned at each other.

"Are you thinking what I'm thinking?" Noah asked.

"I think so!" cried Millie.

"Cookies!" they said together excitedly.

Noah and Millie's grandma made the best chocolate chip cookies. Her cookies always made the two children smile and they knew that their friends would be happy with a plate of cookies too.

"Let's ask Mom to take us to Grandma's house," Millie said.

"After baking, let's pack the cookies in a special box," Noah agreed.

Since they were supposed to go to an amusement park, the two children decided to decorate a box with drawings of popcorn stands, merry-go-rounds, game booths, and more.

When they asked Mom to accompany them to their grandparents' house, she agreed right away.

"I need to drop off some stuff for Grandpa anyway," said Mom.

So off they went. Grandpa and Grandma's house was close to theirs, so they got there in just a few minutes. Once there, the two children hopped out of their car and ran inside.

"Hello, my dears! Mom told me that we have a very important job today," Grandma said with a smile.

"Yes!" Noah exclaimed.

"We're on a mission to make our friends happy," Millie explained.

Right away, Grandma went with the two children to the kitchen. She had already prepared all of the ingredients for her famous chocolate chip cookies. Everything was on the kitchen countertop.

Noah, Millie, and Grandma hummed while they worked. The two children loved baking with Grandma! After preparing the cookies and placing them in the oven, Noah and Millie went to the living room to prepare their special box.

Since the two children had already planned what they wanted to draw, they got to work right away. Noah did the drawings while Millie started coloring and painting. As they worked, the smell of cookies came from the kitchen.

"They're ready!" Grandma said cheerfully.

She walked into the living room carrying a tray filled with freshly baked cookies. Grandma sat next to the two children, then helped them place the cookies in the decorated box.

When they were done, all but two cookies were nicely tucked inside the box.

"What a perfect box! It left two cookies. One for you and one for you," Grandma said as she handed the last two cookies to each of the children.

After eating, they walked up and down the neighborhood. They knocked on the doors of their friends' houses and shared the cookies with them. Each friend they shared their cookies with thanked them happily.

When their box of cookies was empty, Noah and Millie both felt very happy. Since they'd started working together that morning, the two children had learned some very important lessons. They'd learned how important it is to find new ways to make their friends happy.

Then with Grandma's help, they had baked a batch of delicious cookies to share with their friends. At the end of the day, the two children felt great! And they knew that their friends felt happy too.

THE PLAYGROUND BUDDIES

Noah and Millie loved making new friends. If they met other children, they didn't hesitate to talk to them. Since they were kind and liked to make others happy, everyone enjoyed being with them.

They knew almost all of the children in their neighborhood, and they were quite popular in school too. Every weekend, the two children went to different places all over town. They enjoyed meeting their friends in other parts of the town where they played and had fun.

One Saturday morning, Noah and Millie decided to go to the playground at the park.

The playground was one of their favorite places because they could always have fun there. It was often full of children from their school and the rest of the town. Even if they were the only ones there, they still enjoyed using their imaginations to bring the playground to life.

"Look, Noah. There are some kids here today," Millie noticed as they walked toward the playground.

"Are they kids from school? Or are they from our neighborhood?" wondered the little boy.

Millie looked closer and shook her head, "I don't think we know them. Which means that we're about to make some new friends!"

The two children ran toward the playground excitedly and were quite surprised to see the four children playing there. They all looked different from each other!

One little boy had pale skin, straight black hair, and small eyes. He was also wearing a pair of thick glasses. When he grinned at Noah and Millie, his eyes became even smaller. The other little boy had caramel-colored skin, wavy brown hair, and bright green eyes. Instead of smiling, he just looked away and continued playing.

There were two little girls too. One had pale skin, bright red hair, and green eyes. She grinned at Millie warmly. The other little girl had very dark skin, curly black hair, and dark brown eyes. She walked up to Noah and Millie, then waved at them.

"Hi! My name is Maya, and these are my siblings."

The little boy with pale skin and black hair was Tam and the one with wavy brown hair was Ignacio. The little girl with red hair was named Audrey.

"It's nice to meet you! My name is Millie, and this is my brother, Noah."

"Are you new in town?" Noah asked.

"We're just visiting," said Audrey who walked up to Millie and Noah too. "Our parents had to come here for their work, and we asked them if we could come along too."

"We like this town, it's very pretty," said Maya.

"I hope you don't mind me asking, but... are you really siblings? You all look different from each other," Millie noticed.

"You're not the first one to ask us that," Tam said with a chuckle.

"We're adopted," Audrey said with a smile. "Our parents adopted all of us from the same orphanage and we're thankful to them for that. Most grown-ups only adopt one child, but our parents knew that we all wanted to be together."

"They're the best parents in the world," Ignacio said softly, his eyes gleaming in happiness.

"Wow, that's amazing!" Millie exclaimed.

"Can we play with you?" Noah asked.

"Of course!" said the four children cheerfully.

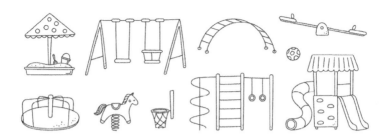

Noah and Millie had a wonderful time playing with Maya, Audrey, Tam, and Ignacio. While playing, their new friends shared stories about their lives in the orphanage. The four children had grown up together and they always felt like they were siblings, not just friends.

When their parents adopted them, they were all very happy!

"What do your parents do for a living?" Noah wondered.

"They visit different schools to talk about diversity. That means being different and learning how to accept those differences," Tam explained.

"That sounds so interesting. And do your parents take you along with them all the time?" asked Millie.

"They often do. Sometimes, they even take us to the schools to introduce us. Then we share our stories with the children in those schools," Audrey answered.

"So... If your parents are here, that means they must be in our school!" Millie exclaimed.

"She's right. There's only one school here in our town," Noah agreed.

"Really? Then we'll ask Mom and Dad if we can visit your school too," Maya said with a grin.

Noah and Millie were happy with the idea. They couldn't wait to introduce their new friends to all of the children in their class. They were glad that they had come to the park. Meeting the four children who looked so different from one another was wonderful!

And the more they played together, the more they got to know Maya, Audrey, Tam, and Ignacio. They discovered some cool things about their new friends that made them realize that making friends is an amazing thing!

THE KINDNESS CLUB

Noah and Millie loved going to school. Millie started going to school first because she was older. When her little brother started going to the same school, the two children had lots of fun!

They enjoyed seeing each other in the halls, and Millie often peeked into Noah's classroom to catch a glimpse of her little brother.

During recess, Noah and Millie often played together. They loved spending time together in the playground, but they also enjoyed playing with their classmates. Since they both started going to school, the two children became closer to each other.

One morning, Noah's teacher made a very exciting announcement.

"Today, we are going to form a Kindness Club," Ms. Jillian said.

"What's that?" Noah asked.

"It's a club that is meant to spread happiness throughout our school. And the best part is, anyone can join!" exclaimed the teacher.

Noah grinned widely. He wanted to tell Millie about the Kindness Club as he knew that she would like to join the club too.

"I made a sign-up sheet, which I will pass around now. Write your name if you would like to be part of the Kindness Club. Then I'll post this sign-up sheet outside our classroom. You can tell everyone about the club and invite them to join too," Ms. Jillian explained.

When the sign-up sheet reached Noah's desk, he wrote his name down happily. And during recess, he quickly ran to Millie's classroom to invite her to join too.

"I would love to join!" Millie exclaimed.

So, she followed her brother back to his classroom to write her name on the sign-up sheet for the Kindness Club.

At the end of the day, the piece of paper was full of names. This made Ms. Jillian very happy! Then she announced that they would have their first meeting the next day.

On their way home, Noah and Millie talked about the new club that they had joined.

"I can't wait to help spread happiness around the school," Millie said. "I wonder what Ms. Jillian will ask us to do."

"Maybe we can think of some activities to share with Ms. Jillian," Noah suggested.

"That's a great idea! We could... help all of the teachers by cleaning the blackboards at the start of the day. That way, they can begin their day with a clean blackboard to write on," Millie said.

"Wow! I'm sure the teachers would love that! To make our school more beautiful, maybe we can all spend time tending to the gardens. Ever since the school gardener left, the plants don't look too healthy anymore," Noah commented.

"You're right! Let's share our ideas with Ms. Jillian tomorrow," said Millie.

The next day, Millie joined Noah, Ms. Jillian, and the rest of the members of the Kindness Club in the Science Lab.

"Thank you all for being here. I am so happy that there are so many of us in this Kindness Club! We are here to perform small acts of kindness around the school so that we can spread happiness to everyone," Ms. Jillian explained. "Now, does anyone have any ideas?"

Right away, Noah and Millie shared their ideas for kind acts. Ms. Jillian and the other members of the Kindness Club loved their ideas, and soon, everyone else shared their thoughts.

Ms. Jillian wrote everything down and when they were done, she said, "You are all amazing! We now have many things to do. Let's start with Noah and Millie's ideas since they were the first ones to share. Then we can go through the other suggestions so that we can spread happiness all over our school."

Noah and half of the Kindness Club went to the garden to tend to the plants while Millie and the other half of the club went into the different classrooms to clean the blackboards.

Gardening and cleaning were hard work! But Noah, Millie, and their friends in the Kindness Club all enjoyed what they were doing. While they worked, other children watched too. Some of them even asked about joining the club because they wanted to help out.

After cleaning the blackboards, all of the teachers thanked Millie and her friends. The teachers also thanked Noah and his friends when they finished sprucing up the garden.

"I am so proud of all of you," said Ms. Jillian. "You all worked hard and made our school a better place. If we keep going, we're sure to make lots of good changes here in our school!"

THE FORGIVING DANDELION

Noah and Millie knew almost everyone who lived in their neighborhood. They knew all the other children who lived there, since most of them went to the same school. Everyone was kind and helped each other out when needed. The two siblings were happy to be part of this neighborhood and greeted their neighbors politely whenever they met.

But the person who lived in the house next door was a mystery to Noah and Millie. They knew that someone lived there, but they had never met that person before.

The two children also knew that their next-door neighbor loved plants because they had a lovely garden outside the house.

"The next-door neighbor must have the greenest thumb in the world," Millie commented while she was playing with Noah in their garden one morning.

"What do you mean?" Noah wondered.

"Well, my teacher said that people who are good at keeping plants alive have a green thumb. Just look at the garden next door, it's beautiful! So, our neighbor must have the greenest thumb ever," explained the little girl.

Then the two children continued to play. Mom had just bought them a new soccer ball and they were kicking it all over their garden. Noah and Millie were having lots of fun until Noah kicked the ball too hard.

Millie thought that the ball was going to hit her face, so she dodged away. But then the ball bounced all the way to the neighbor's garden! It bounced and bounced, and bounced until it landed in their neighbor's dandelion patch.

"Oh, no," Millie whispered with wide eyes as she watched their soccer ball crush the pretty little dandelion flowers.

The yellow dandelions were crushed flat while the fuzzy dandelions lost all of their fluffs. Noah and Millie watched in horror as the dandelion fluffs flew in the wind.

"That's not good," Noah said worriedly. "What do we do now?"

"Well, we have to go there and knock on our neighbor's door. Remember what Mom always tells us. When we do something wrong, even if we didn't do it on purpose, we need to own up to our mistakes and apologize," Millie reminded her brother.

"But we have never met our neighbor before. What if the person who lives there is really mean?" Noah asked in a scared voice.

"We still have to go there and apologize, Noah," Millie said gently. Then she took her brother's hand and said, "Come on, we'll go together."

Noah nodded as his sister took his hand. Then the two children walked over to their neighbor's house. They walked up to the door and knocked on it. Both Noah and Millie felt anxious, but they didn't run away. They knew what they had to do.

A few moments later, the two children heard someone walking toward the door. Then it opened and they saw a little old lady standing in the doorway. She was smiling at them warmly.

"Well, hello there!" said the little old lady cheerfully.

"Hello. My name is Millie, and this is my brother, Noah."

"It's lovely to meet you, Millie and Noah. My name is Ruth. What brings you here to my home?" asked the little old lady.

At first, the two children didn't say anything. Even though their neighbor looked friendly, they still felt worried.

Then Millie took a deep breath and said, "We're sorry, but we ruined your dandelions."

"Oh!" cried Ruth as she glanced at her plants. "What happened?"

This time, Noah spoke up. He told Ruth about how they were playing and how their ball bounced from their garden onto the dandelion plants.

"We didn't mean to ruin your plants. We're very sorry," Noah said.

Ruth looked at Noah and Millie for a moment. Then she smiled kindly and said, "Thank you for coming here and apologizing. You are such sweet little children for doing that. While I do feel sad that my dandelions are gone, I appreciate your honesty and courage."

"Does this mean that you forgive us?" Noah asked softly.

"Of course. After all, you didn't mean to destroy the dandelions," Ruth assured them gently.

"Still, we feel bad about what happened. Is there any way we can make up for what we did?" Millie wondered.

Ruth thought about the little girl's question for a while. Then she smiled and said, "You can help me plant new seeds in that plot of land. But before that, we need to pull out the crushed dandelions. Would you be okay with that?"

"Of course!" exclaimed Noah and Millie together.

The two children went back to their house for a while to ask permission from Mom. Then they spent the rest of the morning helping Ruth in her garden. They learned an important lesson in forgiveness, and they even learned how to plant seeds!

ONTO THE NEXT ADVENTURE...

Do you enjoy spending time with your friends too?

These stories were all about how Noah and Millie had fun adventures with their friends while learning some important lessons along the way. They showed the true meaning of kindness, which made their friends love them even more.

Next up, it's time for some brave escapades that will surely keep you on the edge of your seat!

Chapter 4

Brave Escapades in the Neighborhood

THE MYSTERIOUS MISSING KEY

N oah and Millie were well-known in their neighborhood. They knew most of their neighbors. They even knew the old lady who lived next door, the one who had a beautiful garden outside her house. As they were kind and caring children, everyone appreciated them very much.

Across the street from their house lived another old lady. Her name was Mrs. Johnson, and she always gave plates of freshly baked oatmeal cookies to Noah and Millie whenever she baked some for her grandchildren.

The two children really liked Mrs. Johnson as she also shared stories with them whenever they walked by her house.

"You two remind me so much of my grandchildren," she often said.

Mrs. Johnson's grandchildren lived in another town. But they did visit her once in a while. Noah and Millie had met Mrs. Johnson's grandchildren once. They were very nice and friendly.

One morning, Millie decided to go to the park to see if any of her friends were there. Noah had a big project to finish, and Dad was helping him out. Since she couldn't play with her brother, the little girl hoped that she could meet some of her friends.

But as she walked across their garden, she saw Mrs. Johnson outside her house. The old lady was holding a bag in one hand, and it looked quite heavy. Millie also noticed that Mrs. Johnson had a worried look on her face.

So, the little girl went across the street to check on their neighbor. If something was wrong, she wanted to offer to help as that is what their parents had taught them.

"Good morning, Mrs. Johnson. Are you alright?" she asked.

The old lady turned around in surprise. When she saw Millie, she smiled and said, "Oh, hello Millie. Good morning to you too. Although my morning isn't very good right now."

"Why? What's happened?" asked the little girl worriedly.

"Well, I went out this morning to buy some groceries. My grandchildren are visiting me this weekend, you see. They're arriving tonight and I wanted to cook for them," Mrs. Johnson explained. "I bought more than I expected, and I had to carry this heavy bag home with me. Now, I can't find my key!"

"Oh, dear. No wonder you're just standing out here in your garden," Millie said. "I can help you find your key. While I go looking, I think it would be a good idea to place that heavy bag on your doorstep."

Millie took the bag of groceries from the old lady. Mrs. Johnson was right, it was very heavy! Then the little girl placed it on Mrs. Johnson's doorstep.

"Now, which path did you take when you went into town?"

"I walked down that street," Mrs. Johnson said while pointing to one of the streets. "That's the fastest way to the town, so I also came back the same way."

"Okay," said Millie. "Why don't you continue looking around here while I try to pass along the same street you took going to and from town? Maybe you dropped your key somewhere along the way."

"How nice of you!" said Mrs. Johnson happily. "But is it okay for you to help me? Didn't you have somewhere to go? It seems like you're dressed up to go to the park."

"I was planning to go to the park since Noah is busy today. But the park can wait. I can help you first," Millie assured her.

Then the little girl followed the street that Mrs. Johnson had taken that morning. While walking, Millie looked around. She was hoping to spot Mrs. Johnson's key, which was small and shiny.

Moments later, Millie spotted something on the ground that looked familiar. It was a keychain with a shiny golden elephant on it. She picked it up and looked at it closely.

"Oh, this is Mrs. Johnson's keychain!" she exclaimed. "No wonder it looks so familiar."

Mrs. Johnson had shown the keychain to Noah and Millie the day she got it. Her grandchildren had given the keychain to her as a gift. After seeing the keychain on the ground, Millie knew that the key should be around there too.

The little girl knelt down next to a patch of grass on the side of the street. She reached her hand out and searched for the key in the grass. Soon, she saw something shiny hiding in the green grass.

"There you are!" she said happily.

She picked up the key and brushed the soil off it. Millie thought that Mrs. Johnson must have dropped the keychain and when it fell on the ground, the hook broke off, and the key bounced into the patch of grass.

Thanks to Millie's persistence, she was able to find the old lady's key. So, she walked back to Mrs. Johnson's house feeling pleased and happy for the old lady.

THE DARING RESCUE OPERATION

Noah and Millie loved animals. Ever since they were little, they were interested in learning everything they could about animals. And when they were old enough, they asked their parents if they could have a pet. Some of their friends had pets, and they had played with their friends' pets at times.

Mom and Dad knew that the two children were very responsible, so they agreed. But they first had to decide what pet to get. Millie wanted either a puppy or an iguana while Noah wanted either a hamster or a turtle.

"You need to decide which pet to get," Dad said. "That way, we will know where to go to find the pet you want."

"We should get a pet that we both like," Millie said. "How about... a cat?"

"Hmmmm...," Noah said. "I guess that would be okay."

"Cats are soft and fluffy like puppies and hamsters. And we can choose a cat that's not too big so it would be like having a small dog or a big hamster. What do you think?" Millie asked.

"I think we've found our perfect pet," Noah agreed with a grin.

So, they went to the shelter to find a cat that needed a new home. After looking at the cats in the different cages, the two children found one that they both wanted to take home. They named the cat Whiskers, and they loved him ever since.

One day, while Millie was at her best friend's house, Noah took Whiskers out to explore the neighborhood. Everything was going fine until a car beeped its horn loudly! Whiskers screeched and ran up a tree.

"Oh no!" cried Noah as he watched his pet scramble up and sit on one of the branches.

He tried calling Whiskers down, but the cat wouldn't move. Noah knew that he had to save his pet. The little boy could climb up the tree, but he wouldn't be able to climb down while carrying Whiskers.

So, he looked around to see if there was something he could use. He saw one of his friends playing in their yard. It looked like he was practicing party tricks as he was pulling several colorful scarves out of his sleeve.

Just then, Noah had a great idea. He walked over to his friend's yard.

"Hi, Noah!" said the little boy whose name was Shane.

"Hello, Shane. Are you practicing your party tricks? I saw you pulling these scarves from out of your sleeve. That was really cool!" Noah exclaimed.

"Thank you, Noah! I'm practicing because my cousins are visiting us next week and I wanted to show them my new party tricks," Shane explained. "By the way, what are you doing here?"

"I came over to ask for your help. My cat is stuck in a tree, and I need to borrow your scarves. Is that okay?"

"Sure! I can even come with you in case you need more help," Shane offered.

Noah thanked his friend, and together, they went to the tree where Whiskers was stuck. After listening to Noah's plan, Shane helped him tie the scarves together to form a big square. Then Noah thanked his friend and climbed up the tree.

"I'm coming, Whiskers," he said.

Noah enjoyed climbing trees with Millie, so he felt quite confident. When he reached the branch where Whiskers was, he reached out to the cat. Whiskers purred and walked toward Noah.

"Good job, Whiskers," he said.

Then he tied the scarves around his pet's body as a makeshift parachute. When he was done, he looked down to check if Shane was in position.

"Whiskers is ready! Are you ready too, Shane?"

"Yes, I am!" Shane called back.

"Don't worry, Whiskers. You'll be fine," Noah assured his pet.

Then he stretched his arms out and let go of Whiskers. Just like he planned, Whiskers slowly fell from the tree and into Shane's waiting arms.

"I got him!" Shane called out.

"Great! I'm coming back down," Noah said, then he carefully climbed down the tree.

Once he was on the ground, he untied the scarves from around Whisker's body. Then he and Shane untied the scarves from each other.

When they were done, Noah said, "Thank you for lending me your scarves. And thank you for helping me save Whiskers."

"You're welcome, Noah. You were so brave! Even though climbing the tree was risky, you did it bravely so that you could save your pet," Shane said with a grin.

Noah smiled at his friend, then hugged his pet. He was just glad that everything had turned out perfectly.

The Great Garden Challenge

Noah and Millie always had bright ideas, even when things didn't seem great. They liked to think of ways to make their lives better. They also liked to use their ideas to help other people out.

One morning, while Noah and Millie were walking around their neighborhood, the little girl stopped and sighed.

"What's wrong?" Noah wondered.

"It's this place," Millie said while looking at the empty lot in front of her. Their neighborhood was a beautiful place except for one empty lot that was dirty and brown.

"I know that nobody owns this lot. But I wish we could do something to make it more beautiful," she said.

"I know what you mean. I heard Mom say one time that this was an eyesore. When I asked her what that meant, she said that it was something that didn't look good," Noah said. "But what can we do?"

"Do you remember when a lady visited us to ask Mom to show the neighbors how to beautify their mailboxes?" Millie asked.

"Do you mean the lady from the... Homeowners Asso... what was that word?"

"That's right!" Millie exclaimed. "The lady was from the Homeowners Association. Maybe Mom or Dad can talk to them about making this lot more beautiful."

So, Noah and Millie talked to their parents. Mom agreed to talk to the Homeowners Association. To the delight of the two children, the Homeowners Association decided to host a contest to make the lot more beautiful.

While Noah visited one of his friends, Millie watched as the people from the Homeowners Association prepared the lot. They decided to have a gardening competition for the children in the neighborhood. To prepare, they divided the lot into sections so each contestant could make their part of the lot more attractive.

Of course, Millie signed up for the competition. It was her idea, after all! As she watched them prepare, the little girl felt excited.

On the day of the competition, Millie came prepared. Dad, Mom, and Noah came to watch the competition and support Millie. The little girl brought a wagon filled with plants, flowers, and garden ornaments.

"Is everyone ready?" asked the lady from the Homeowners Association. "Let's begin!"

Millie got to work right away. She knew exactly what she wanted to do as she had been planning since she signed up. She planted the plants and flowers in the soil, then added some garden ornaments around them.

The little girl was proud of how her patch of land turned out. Millie had a green thumb, so she liked to help Mom with their garden back home. She was the one who had planted and cared for all of the plants and flowers that she used for the competition.

When the little girl was finished, she looked around. She saw that all the other children who had joined the gardening competition were working hard to make their plot of land green and beautiful.

"You did this," Mom said gently.

Millie looked up and saw Mom standing next to her. She stood up and asked, "What do you mean?"

"For the longest time, I only saw this empty lot as an eyesore," Mom said. "I think everyone thought the same thing. But instead of just leaving it alone, you thought of a way to make this place beautiful. I am proud of you, Millie."

"Thanks, Mom," said the little girl shyly.

Mom walked back to where Noah and Dad were standing. As for Millie, she watched all the other children work hard on their plots of land. It was quite a sight to see! What used to be a dreary and dirty place was now changing into something colorful and alive.

When the competition was over, the judges walked around to see all of the plots of land. They stopped when they reached Millie's area.

"How beautiful!" exclaimed one of the judges. "Did you plant all of these plants yourself?"

"Yes," Millie answered with a smile. "We have a garden outside our house, and I have been helping my mom grow different kinds of plants in it. I only took the plants and flowers that I grew and cared for."

"Well then, I think we have a winner," said the head judge.

Of course, everyone agreed as Millie's plot of land was the most beautiful one. As Millie listened to everyone cheering for her, she discovered something important. Putting a lot of time and effort into projects is important, especially if you want to succeed.

The Friendly Neighborhood Cleanup

Noah and Millie cared deeply about their neighborhood. After Millie had won a gardening competition that changed the empty lot in their neighborhood from a sad place to a beautiful one, they were on the lookout for their next project.

"Our neighborhood is so awesome now," Noah said as they walked by the lot that was filled with beautiful plants and flowers.

"I'm proud of all our friends. I see them come here to water the plants and tend to the gardens sometimes," Millie said.

"So, what do we do next?" Noah asked.

"I don't know yet. We just have to keep finding ways to make our community a better place," Millie said.

The two children kept walking until they reached the park. As soon as they got there, Noah stopped.

He grabbed Millie's arm and said, "I think I know what our next project should be."

"What?" Millie wondered.

"Take a look at the park. It used to be so clean. But now, it has so much litter and clutter," Noah said.

"Oh, you're right," Millie agreed. "I don't know why I never noticed that before. But we can't talk to the Homeowners Association this time. They only handle problems with our neighborhood."

"We don't need their help. We can just talk to our friends at school," Noah said with a grin.

"If you think that you can lead this project, then I will support you all the way," Millie said.

The next day, at school, Noah talked to his teacher, Ms. Jillian.

"My sister and I went to the park yesterday and we saw that there was so much litter everywhere. So, we decided to invite our friends and classmates to have a cleanup drive. Would it be okay for me to make an announcement to everyone?"

"Of course, Noah! That is such a wonderful idea," Ms. Jillian said.

When the bell rang and everyone sat down, Ms. Jillian asked Noah to come to the front of the classroom. Once there, he thanked Ms. Jillian, then faced his classmates. The little boy told them about what he had noticed in the playground, then he shared his idea.

"I'll join the cleanup drive," said Jonathan, Noah's best friend.

"Thanks," Noah said.

Then everyone else in the class agreed to join the cleanup drive too. During recess, Noah ran to his sister's classroom to tell her the good news. Before he could reach her classroom, he ran into her in the hallway.

"I was just coming to see you!" Millie exclaimed. "Everyone in my class will join your cleanup drive."

"That's amazing!" Noah exclaimed. "Everyone in my class will join too."

"So, when do you want to do the cleanup drive?" Millie asked.

"This Saturday. I'll ask Mom and Dad to prepare everything we need," Noah said.

For the rest of the week, Noah and Millie helped their parents plan and prepare for the cleanup drive. When the day finally came, Mom and Dad went with the two children to the park. They wanted to help out too.

All of Noah and Millie's classmates arrived at the park on time. Together with his parents, sister, and friends, Noah collected all of the trash and placed the recyclables in the recycling bin. They even brought a bin to put compost in so that they could use the compost to make the neighborhood gardens healthier.

Everyone worked the whole day to create a cleaner and greener space for the whole community to enjoy. They only took a break for lunch. Mom prepared delicious meals for everyone, and they all enjoyed eating together.

After lunch, they went back to work. At the end of the day, Noah felt proud of what they had done. The park was totally free of litter, and it looked beautiful as it did before.

"Thank you, everyone. I'm sure that the people from our community will be surprised when they come to the park tomorrow. I just hope that they will also take care of our park from now on," Noah said.

When everyone left, Noah realized something important. Taking responsibility for the environment is something that everyone should do. He learned that by doing something and inviting others to help out, we can make a positive change in the community.

With his family and friends, Noah was able to create a cleaner and more enjoyable environment for everyone.

Onto the Next Adventure...

Do you think that you can be brave just like Noah and Millie?

These stories were all about how Noah and Millie thought of amazing ideas and used those ideas to solve problems, help other people, and inspire great change. Even small things can have big effects, so don't be afraid to share your ideas and think of ways to make life better!

Now, let's hear some stories about family and love...

Chapter 5

Family and Love

THE SURPRISE PARTY

N oah and Millie loved each other dearly. Millie was the big sister and Noah was her little brother. Millie took good care of her brother, and she always wanted him to be happy.

One morning, while talking to Mom, the little girl suddenly had a great idea.

"Mom, do you think we could throw a surprise party for Noah?" Millie asked.

"That's a wonderful idea!" Mom exclaimed.

"Thanks," said the little girl with a grin. "Can you please help me plan his party?"

"Of course," Mom said. "You can be the party planner and I will be your helper."

Since Noah was at the mall with Dad, Millie and Mom were able to share their ideas for Noah's party. The little boy loved dinosaurs, so they decided to make it a Dino Party!

"I'll take Noah to the mall this weekend to buy dinosaur-themed clothes for him," Mom said.

"While you're at the mall, Dad and I can work together to make the decorations," the little girl suggested.

"That's a great idea!" Mom exclaimed. "What decorations do you plan to make?"

"I remember that we have a party box, right?" Millie asked. "Can we check what's inside so that I can think about other decorations to make with Dad?"

"Another great idea," Mom said with a smile.

So, Mom and Millie went to the attic to find the party box. Mom found the box and opened it. They were delighted to see green and blue streamers inside. They also saw some big, colorful letters they could use to spell NOAH and DINO PARTY.

Millie continued to rummage through the box. At the bottom, she found some colorful tablecloths. She took the blue, green, and brown-colored tablecloths and placed the rest back inside the box.

"I think we have everything we need," Millie said and Mom agreed.

"We also need to make invitations to give to Noah's friends. You can give the invitations a few days before his DINO Party, but make sure that Noah doesn't see you," Mom said. "We can also ask Grandma and Grandpa to help out."

The next day, Mom dropped Millie off at their grandparents' house.

"Why can't I go to Grandma and Grandpa's house too?" Noah wondered.

"You promised to come with me to the pet store to buy food and other supplies for Whiskers, remember? And we should always keep our promises, right?" Mom reminded the little boy.

"I'll see you later, Noah!" Millie said cheerfully as Mom and Noah dropped her off.

Then the little girl ran into her grandparents' house.

"Hello, Grandma," she said with a smile when her grandma opened the door.

"Hello, dear," Grandma said. "Come in, we have a lot to talk about."

Millie hugged her grandma, then went inside. They went to the kitchen where Grandma prepared snacks for them to share while planning. As soon as they sat down, they talked about Noah's party.

Grandma said, "I can bake cookies for everyone. Grandpa said that he can prepare anything you need for the games. He also went to the mall to buy candies and toys for Noah's goodie bags."

"Wow! We'll be doing so many things!" Millie said.

Grandma smiled and Millie told her about the plans that she had thought of with Mom. They wrote everything down in Millie's notebook. For the next few days, Millie planned and prepared for Noah's party with the help of Mom, Dad, Grandma, and Grandpa.

When the special day came, Millie was very excited. After sharing a delicious breakfast as a family, Mom took Noah out for a while. As soon as they left, Millie and Dad were off to work on party preparations. They started decorating the house.

A few minutes later, Grandma and Grandpa arrived too. They brought a lot of stuff for the party! By working together, they were able to make the backyard the perfect place for a Dino Party.

Soon, Noah's friends arrived too. Millie led them to the backyard and asked them to find a place to hide. When the little boy came back with Mom, he wondered where his sister was. He searched all over the house but couldn't find her.

"Where is Millie?" he wondered.

Then he decided to check the backyard. What he didn't know was that Mom had been following him all along. When he opened the door to the backyard, Millie jumped up along with everyone else and yelled, "SURPRISE!"

"Wow!" Noah exclaimed. "Thank you so much!"

His face was a picture! He'd never had a surprise party before and was so happy.

Millie was happy that the party was a success. She knew that her brother felt all of the love and appreciation they had for him as they celebrated his very special day.

The Family Talent Show

Noah and Millie were cheerful and confident children who really liked joining activities at school. They were both very talented and they weren't afraid to share their talents with other people.

Noah could play different musical instruments too. His favorite instrument was the guitar, and he was really good at playing it. The little boy had been interested in music since he was very young.

He was also very interested in musical instruments. So, Mom and Dad bought different musical instruments for him to try. They got him a pair of maracas, a small piano, a flute, and a guitar. Although he was able to play the different instruments, the guitar was Noah's favorite.

Millie was very talented too. She loved to sing and had a beautiful voice. All of her relatives enjoyed listening to her sing whenever they had family gatherings. She also enjoyed singing in front of other people, because she liked to see the smiles on their faces after every song.

One morning, at school, Noah and Millie felt very excited. All of the students gathered at the auditorium and the principal had a very exciting announcement.

"In two weeks, we will have a Family Talent Show," the principal said. "Everyone can join! You can share your talent as a family, or each member of the family can also share their talent individually. The choice is yours."

After the announcement, the principal asked the children to go back to their classes and go about their day. Noah and Millie went to their classrooms and listened to their teachers. When the class was over, they met in the playground, then walked together to where Dad picked them up.

"Dad! You won't believe what our principal said!" Noah exclaimed.

"What was that?" Dad wondered.

"We're going to have a Family Talent Show in two weeks," Millie replied excitedly.

"Wow! That's great news!" Dad exclaimed.

Then they talked about the different talents they had while they walked home. Once there, the whole family went to the kitchen to share the good news with Mom.

"That's so exciting! What talents should we show?" Mom asked.

"I'll play the guitar, of course," Noah said proudly.

"And I'll sing my favorite song," said Millie with a smile.

"Perfect!" Mom exclaimed. Then she turned to Dad and asked, "Will you share your super secret special talent?"

Noah and Millie's eyes grew wide as they stared at Dad. Then Millie asked, "You have a super secret special talent?"

"What is it?" Noah asked.

Instead of answering, Dad grinned. Then he picked up three oranges from the fruit basket on the kitchen counter and started juggling them!

"Wow! I didn't know you could do that!" Noah cried happily.

With a giggle, Millie said, "That is a super special talent! But it's not a secret now!"

Dad caught the three oranges in his hands and grinned. Then he looked at Mom and asked, "How about you? What will you do?"

The two children looked at their mom hopefully. They wondered if Mom had a super secret special talent too. Mom thought about it for a moment, then said, "I think I can decorate a cake for the show. Do you think that would be a nice talent to share?"

"Yes!" Millie exclaimed.

Grandma was a wonderful baker and she taught Mom how to bake too, and Mom learned how to decorate cakes beautifully.

"Now that we have all decided what talents to share, it's time for us to practice," Dad said.

For the next two weeks, Dad, Mom, Noah, and Millie practiced their talents. They took turns showing each other what they planned to perform at the talent show. They also helped each other make their performances better.

When it was time for the Family Talent Show, they were all ready and excited. Mom went up first and she amazed everyone with her cake decorating talent. Dad went next and everyone cheered as he juggled different objects.

Noah went next. He played one of Mom's favorite songs on his guitar. When he was done, Mom wiped tears of joy from her eyes. The last member of the family to perform was Millie who sang a beautiful song for everyone.

As each member of the family performed, they felt proud of themselves. They also felt closer to one another as they supported each other while practicing and on the special day too.

"Congratulations, Noah! Congratulations, Millie!" Mom exclaimed after the two children performed.

"You two did so well," Dad said proudly.

"We all did well," Millie said with a smile.

"Congratulations to us!" exclaimed Noah, who felt just as happy as his sister for being able to share in such a special event with his parents.

THE CAMPING ADVENTURE

As Noah and Millie were adventurous children who loved the outdoors, one of their favorite activities was camping. They had only been camping with Mom and Dad once. They had so much fun that time that they were now eagerly looking forward to their next camping trip.

To their delight, Mom and Dad told them that they would be going on another camping trip at the weekend.

"And the best part is, Grandma and Grandpa are joining us," Dad said with a grin.

"Wow! That's so exciting!" Millie clapped her hands cheerfully.

"I want to sleep next to Grandpa!" Noah exclaimed.

"I'm sure he would love that," Mom said while laughing softly.

Even though the camping trip was still a few days away, Noah and Millie started packing their things. Having been on a camping trip once, they already knew what they needed to take.

In the next few days, Noah and Millie kept talking about their camping trip. They had lots of plans and ideas for how to make it the best camping trip ever. They wanted the trip to be extra special because their grandparents were going to join them.

When the day of the camping trip finally came, the two children woke up extra early. They made their beds, brushed their teeth, and got dressed. Then they ran to their parents' room to wake them up.

"Mom! Dad! Today is the day!" they cried as they burst into their parents' room.

"Oh! You're too late," said Dad with a big grin as he finished making his bed. "Mom and I woke up very early to prepare. She's in the dining room now, preparing breakfast. Also, Grandma just called a few moments ago and she said that they're on their way."

Noah and Millie jumped up excitedly, then they ran to the dining room to greet Mom. She greeted them back and said, "I've prepared a hearty meal for everyone. Eat up. Grandma and Grandpa will be here soon."

"Dad has just finished making the bed so I'm sure he'll be here soon," Millie said.

The two children sat down and thanked Mom for their food. Mom prepared big breakfast plates with waffles, eggs, bacon, and a small bowl of sliced fruits. She also gave Noah and Millie a glass of milk each.

While the two children were eating, Dad and Mom joined them. Moments later, their grandparents arrived and joined them too.

"Are you ready to spend the day in the great outdoors?" Grandma asked.

Noah and Millie nodded as their mouths were full.

"And are you ready to sleep in the great outdoors?" asked Grandpa.

"Yes!" exclaimed Noah and Millie together.

After breakfast, everyone loaded their things in the family car. Then they all got in. It was a bit crowded, but Noah and Millie didn't mind. They were just happy and excited to be going on a trip with their parents and grandparents.

As soon as they arrived at the campsite, Dad and Grandpa pitched the tent. Noah and Millie helped them out since they'd already learned how to pitch a tent the last time they went camping.

While they worked, Mom and Grandma prepared everything else. When all of their things were ready, the whole family kicked off their fun camping trip with a walk around the campsite.

They saw some interesting plants, cute little animals, and they even met other campers along the way.

After their walk, Dad started a campfire so that they could roast hotdogs and marshmallows. While enjoying their campfire treats, the two children and their parents had fun listening to stories from Grandma and Grandpa.

They talked about how they lived their lives in the past and how things have changed so much since then. Noah and Millie thought that their grandparents' stories were so interesting!

After filling themselves up on roasted hotdogs and marshmallows, the family played some outdoor games. Mom, Millie, and Grandma formed one team while Dad, Noah, and Grandpa formed their own team. They were all so good at the games that they ended up in a tie.

"This means that we're all winners!" Grandma exclaimed.

The two children cheered happily as they loved to win! It had been such a fun-filled day that they didn't notice how late it was. The sun had already started to set, so Mom and Grandma started preparing dinner.

The whole family enjoyed their dinner together, then they lay down on mats to watch the stars. The two children were tired but happy. They enjoyed the camping trip so much as they were able to spend quality time together as a family.

THE FAMILY RECIPE

Noah and Millie loved their grandparents very much. They enjoyed making happy memories with their parents. But they also loved spending time with their Grandma and Grandpa.

The two children often went to their grandparents' house during weekends. Whenever they visited, Grandma and Grandpa always prepared fun activities for them to do.

One morning, while having breakfast, Mom's phone rang. She excused herself for a minute and walked out of the dining room to answer her phone. Moments later, she came back with a smile on her face.

"Who was that?" Dad asked.

"It was Mom. She wants Noah and Millie to visit them. She said that she has something very special for them to do," Mom explained. Then she turned to the two children and asked, "Do you two want to visit Grandma and Grandpa today?"

"Yes, please!" Noah and Millie replied.

So, they quickly finished their meals and went to their rooms to get changed. After that, Dad drove the two children to their grandparents' house.

"Bye, Dad!" Noah called out as he hopped out of the car and ran up to Grandma and Grandpa's house.

"See you later, Dad," Millie said, then she gave Dad a kiss before hopping out of the car and following her brother.

The door was already open, so Millie went inside.

"There you are, dear! Come in, join Noah, Grandpa, and me in the kitchen," Grandma said.

Millie felt curious as she followed her grandmother to the kitchen. Once there, she saw Grandpa and Noah sitting at the kitchen table with a bunch of ingredients in front of them.

"What's all this?" Millie wondered.

"Come and sit down first," said Grandma. So, the little girl did as she was told.

"This morning, Grandma and I were rummaging through the attic. We were looking for some albums that we wanted to give to your parents. But instead, we found your grandma's box of recipes," Grandpa explained.

Grandma took a box from the chair next to hers, then she placed it on the table. It was a beautiful brown box with gold linings. Grandma opened the box and showed the two children what was in it.

"Are those pieces of paper?" Noah asked.

"Yes, they are! And each paper contains a treasured family recipe," Grandpa answered.

"You both know how much I love to cook, right? Well, my mother loved to cook too," Grandma said. "She was a wonderful cook! And whenever she created a delicious dish, she wrote the recipe down on a piece of paper. Then she kept all of those recipes in this box and gave them to me when I married your Grandpa."

"Wow, that's such a wonderful story," Millie said.

"So, all of these are recipes from our great grandma?" Noah asked with wide eyes.

"Exactly," Grandma said. "And today, I would like to teach you how to make one of these dishes. This is Grandpa's favorite dish and I just happened to have all of the ingredients for it."

"Cool!" Noah exclaimed.

"I can't wait to start!" Millie said excitedly.

And so they did. First, Grandpa named all of the ingredients in front of them. Some of the ingredients were easy, like salt, pepper, and potatoes. But some of the ingredients weren't familiar to Noah and Millie. They had never cooked with those ingredients before.

Discovering new ingredients made the two children feel even more excited about cooking with their grandparents. After Grandpa named all of the ingredients, Grandma shared the steps of the recipe with them.

She told them what each step was and also explained what they would have to do at each step. When they started, Grandma and Grandpa also talked about their family. Grandma talked about her mother who created all of the recipes. Grandpa talked about his mother too, since she was a great cook as well.

While they cooked, Noah and Millie enjoyed listening to their grandparents' stories. Even though they had never met their great grandparents, they learned about their family's heritage and how important it is to keep family traditions alive.

"It smells so good, Grandma!" Noah said cheerfully as the aroma of their dish wafted around the kitchen.

"Noah's right. That smells wonderful! No wonder Grandpa loves that dish," Millie agreed.

While waiting for their special dish to be ready, Noah and Millie listened to more stories about their grandparents' families. It was a very special day as they learned to appreciate their family's traditions, history, and the love that was shared through the passing down of family stories and recipes.

ONTO THE NEXT ADVENTURE...

Did those stories make you feel all warm and fuzzy inside?

Family is truly important. This is something that Noah and Millie have learned by spending quality time with their parents, grandparents, and, of course, with each other. They have created lovely memories together and those memories will surely stay in Noah and Millie's hearts forever.

Now, let's take a walk in the great outdoors so that you can learn how to appreciate nature more, just like Noah and Millie...

MAKE A DIFFERENCE WITH YOUR REVIEW

"In every child, there is a spark of imagination and wonder. We fan that spark by sharing stories and lightening up the world" – Penelope Arnoll-Davis.

D ear Reader,

There's nothing quite like a bedtime story to transport a child to a world of dreams and adventures. *"Fun Bedtime Stories For Kids Ages 4-8"* was crafted with love and imagination to ensure every reading is an unforgettable journey. But in order to reach children's hearts everywhere, we need your help.

Your book review will bring a little joy and wonder to other parents and children searching for their next beloved story. It's a simple act that can make a real difference by helping:

...one more child to journey through dreams ...one more family to bond over a shared story ...one more classroom to echo with laughter and learning...one more dream to be believed and pursued.

Leaving a review on Amazon is easy and takes less than a minute. Simply scan the QR code below:

USA

For non-US residents choose from one of the QR codes below:

UK

ITALY

AUSTRALIA

CANADA

I'm excited to continue this journey with you. Together, we can make every bedtime a delightful and happy experience, leaving cherished, lasting memories.

With heartfelt thanks,
Penelope Arnoll-Davis

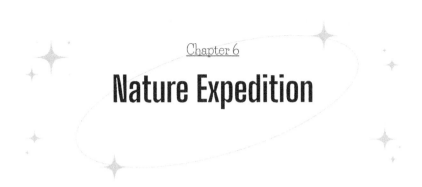

Nature Expedition

The Secret Trail

N oah and Millie loved to spend time exploring nature in their neighborhood and the local park. So, when Mom and Dad told the children that they were going to spend a week at the National Park with their grandparents, they were very excited!

The family arrived at the National Park in the morning. Mom, Dad, Grandpa, and Grandma checked into the hotel, and the two children couldn't wait to explore the park.

"We promise not to leave the park," Millie said. "We just want to explore while you're unpacking. Can we? Please?"

"Okay, you can go." Dad said. "Just stay in the hotel grounds and don't stay out too long. We have a trail hike scheduled for this morning, so you need to be here when we call you."

"Okay," Millie said.

The two children walked out of the hotel. When they'd arrived that morning, they'd seen some amazing tree-lined mountains and a lake. Now, in the hotel grounds, they saw all sorts of different kinds of trees and colorful flowers and plants, and the air smelled so sweet.

"I'm so glad that Mom and Dad brought us here with Grandma and Grandpa," Millie said while breathing in the fresh air.

"Me too. This place is awesome," Noah agreed. "I wonder if there are any animals here."

As Noah and Millie explored the park, they saw other people who were out exploring like them. Everyone they met seemed to be in a good mood as they smiled and greeted the two children cheerfully.

"Everyone here seems so happy and relaxed," Noah observed.

"I think it's because this place is so beautiful. Even I feel happy and relaxed just walking around the park," Millie said with a smile.

After a while, Noah and Millie decided to go back to their hotel. They didn't want to miss the trail hike that their parents had planned for them. When they got to the hotel, they saw their parents and grandparents waiting outside.

"There you are!" Grandpa exclaimed.

"You're right on time," said Mom. "We've finished unpacking everything and are now ready to go."

"Are you ready for our trail hike?" Dad asked.

When Noah and Millie nodded excitedly, Dad continued, "This park has a trail that goes around the whole place. As long as we follow the trail, we can see every part of the park and be back here at the hotel."

As Noah, Millie, and the rest of the family followed the trail, they saw some breathtaking landscapes. Everything around them was beautiful!

The two children were also delighted to spot squirrels and chipmunks scurrying around happily on the grass and in the trees. They even saw some deer in the distance.

While they followed the well-trodden path, Noah and Millie's curious minds took over. They looked around and all of a sudden discovered a hidden trail!

"Look here, everyone!" Noah called out.

"It's a hidden path," Millie said with amazement. "Can we please follow it?"

"I don't see why not," Dad said with a smile.

And so, the whole family explored the hidden path. While walking, they saw some fascinating nooks and secret hideaways. There were even small caves with sparkling gems stuck in the rocky walls.

"Look, there are signs all around," Mom noticed. "I think the owners of the park know about this path, but they don't tell the visitors about it. Maybe it's only for those who can find it."

"Then it's a good thing that our two little detectives found this path for us," Grandma said proudly.

"She's right! If Noah and Millie hadn't found it, we would have carried on along the boring old trail," Grandpa said with a wink.

The two children giggled at their grandpa. They knew that he loved nature just as much as they did. Even if they had kept to the original trail, they were sure that they would have seen more of nature's beauty.

"I think when we've finished exploring this hidden trail, we can go back to the other one. That way, we can truly explore every part of this amazing park," Millie said.

"I agree!" said Noah excitedly.

And so, Noah, Millie, and the rest of their family spent their first day at the National Park exploring every corner to discover how beautiful it truly was.

THE ANIMAL WHISPERS

Noah and Millie were always excited to see animals and birds in the wild. They loved nature and enjoyed exploring new places that had a lot of natural beauty. While they didn't often see animals in their neighborhood, they now had a chance to see many more because they were staying at the hotel in the National Park for a week.

On their first day, they explored the National Park by following a trail that goes all around it. They even discovered a secret trail that took them to amazing hidden places.

"Do you remember the deer we saw near the caves?" Noah asked while he sat with Millie on a low wall outside their hotel.

Mom and Dad were still having breakfast at the restaurant while Grandma and Grandpa had gone for a stroll.

"Yes, those deer were beautiful," Millie said. "But I wonder what they were doing near the caves."

"Maybe the deer were going on an adventure," Noah said.

With a smile, Millie tried to imagine what the two deer would have talked about if they'd wanted to go on an adventure. "We should give them names," she said.

"One of them could be Alex while the other could be Holly," Noah suggested.

"Those are really nice names," said the little girl with a smile. "Now let me try to imagine what they were talking about when they woke up that morning."

And so, the two children used their imaginations to create a story for the two deer, Alex and Holly.

"It's such a beautiful morning today," Holly said. "Do you want to explore the park with me?"

"Of course!" Alex exclaimed. "But... There are so many people in the park during the summer months. Aren't you a little scared of them?"

Holly thought about Alex's question for a while. She did feel uneasy when people came too close to her. But she just loved to walk around the park so much. It was their home and she thought that it was beautiful.

"I think we'll be okay," said Holly. "None of the people we've met have done anything to hurt us. Sure, they come too close to us sometimes. But I think they're just curious."

"I'm curious too, but I would never go near them," said Alex who was feeling a bit worried.

Still, he agreed to explore the park with Holly. He even suggested they could go to the caves since some of the most delicious plants in the park grew in that area. As they walked together, the two deer listened to the sounds of nature, like rustling leaves, birdsong, and the sound of rushing water from a stream nearby.

When they reached the caves, Alex and Holly started munching on the delicious plants. They felt calm and happy until they heard footsteps coming toward them. Feeling a little scared, Alex stopped eating. He raised his head and looked around. Deer are very shy creatures.

Holly didn't feel too worried, but she stopped eating and lifted her head too. Then, out of the trees, came two small children. They didn't look scary at all. In fact, they looked quite friendly!

"Those two children are you and me!" exclaimed Noah. He felt super excited to be part of Millie's story.

Millie giggled, then went back to imagining the story of the two deer.

Alex and Holly stared at the children. They wondered if they should wait for the children to go away so they could go back to munching on the tasty plants, or if it was better to leave.

To Alex's great surprise, Holly began walking slowly toward the two children.

"What are you doing?" he asked worriedly.

"I just want to see them up close," Holly said. "Don't worry. If they move, I'll just run away."

The two small children didn't move. They just watched as Holly walked closer and closer. When she was near enough to see them clearly, Holly stopped. She stared at them.

Noah and Millie were smiling at her and held out their hands offering leaves as a gift. Holly didn't get too close, but when Noah and Millie gently placed the leaves on the ground in front of the deer, everything became clear to Holly, and she knew they were friends.

"You know, Noah," Millie said. "Just seeing that deer walking up to us was amazing. I felt we had a special connection and I think she knew we would never do anything to harm her."

"Yes," said Noah. "All animals are our friends."

NATURE'S SYMPHONY

Noah and Millie knew how to appreciate nature and the world around them. They felt happiest when they were outside, and they loved using their imaginations to make the great outdoors even more fun!

The two children were visiting the National Park for a week and were staying at a hotel, which was a new experience for them.

"I love hearing different kinds of bird sounds every morning when I wake up," Millie commented as she stretched her arms and yawned.

Noah yawned too as he sat up on his bed. He rubbed his eyes and said, "The sounds of nature here are different from the sounds of nature back home."

"Yes, they are so amazing," Millie said with a smile. "And I just had a cool idea."

"What is it?" Noah wondered.

"Come on, let's get dressed while I tell you," said the little girl.

After making their bed, brushing their teeth, and getting dressed, Noah felt very excited about his big sister's idea. They joined their parents and grandparents in the hotel dining room and the whole family enjoyed their breakfast.

When the two children had finished eating, Millie stood up and asked, "Mom, Dad, can Noah and I play outside today?"

"Oh? Do you have anything planned?" Mom asked with a smile.

"Yes!" Noah exclaimed. "Millie and I are going to play music!"

"That sounds wonderful," Grandma said.

So, Mom nodded and the two children ran outside into the hotel grounds.

"Where do we start?" Noah asked.

Millie closed her eyes. She brought her finger up to her lips and said, "Shhhhhh. Listen."

So, Noah followed his big sister. He closed his eyes too and listened. They heard the sound of the soft breeze blowing through the trees. They also heard the sounds of different types of birds.

When Noah opened his eyes, he saw his sister grinning at him. She had picked up two leaves from the ground and she handed one leaf to him.

"What will I do with this?" Noah wondered.

Millie placed the edge of the leaf to her lips, took a deep breath, and blew on it. To Noah's surprise, he heard a high-pitched whistling sound coming from the leaf!

"Wow! Where did you learn how to do that?" asked the little boy excitedly.

"One of my classmates, Sarah, showed me. Then I got the idea of trying to use things in nature to play music," Millie explained. "Now I'll show you."

Noah made a whistling sound at his first try!

"What else can we do?" Noah asked while looking around.

Just then, he had an idea. He picked up two pebbles from the ground and started tapping them against each other. Millie smiled as he played a simple beat using the pebbles. As he played his music, Millie brought the leaf up to her lips once again and started playing music with it.

As they played their music, the two children closed their eyes. They heard the sounds of nature mixed together with the sounds that they were making.

Then they heard other sounds that made both children open their eyes. To their delight, they saw Mom, Dad, Grandpa and Grandma standing near them. Grandpa had picked a fuzzy reed from the plants near their hotel. He brushed the fuzzy reed against the ground to make an interesting sound.

Grandma picked up two large leaves and started swinging them around to make a low whistling noise. The music they made together sounded lovely! Then the two children turned to Mom and Dad.

"Come on, Mom! Join us!" Millie exclaimed.

"You too, Dad!" said Noah cheerfully.

Mom and Dad glanced at each other, then grinned. They looked around for something to use.

"Maybe this will work," Mom said as she picked up some seeds that were scattered on the ground.

She placed the seeds in a plastic cup that she had brought from the hotel, covered the top of the cup with her hand, and started shaking it like a maracas.

"Perfect!" Millie exclaimed.

Dad started humming softly while everyone else played their instruments. After a while, one by one they stopped until only Dad was left. He had a calming voice and the sound of him humming made them all feel relaxed and happy.

That morning, Noah and Millie discovered how wonderful it is to take a moment to listen to the sounds of nature and find peace in the great outdoors.

FAREWELL, NATIONAL PARK

Noah and Millie went on more adventures while at the National Park, and each day brought new surprises. The family spent happy moments together in the company of nature, and now it was their last day at the Park. Noah and Millie were feeling quite sad.

"I can't believe it has been a week already," Noah said with a sigh.

Millie smiled kindly at her brother. She felt the same way. But unlike Noah, she felt happy even though it was their last day.

"I love this place just as much as you, Noah. But in a way, I'm kind of glad we're leaving this afternoon," Millie admitted.

"What? Why?" Noah wondered.

"Well, I miss our home. The National Park is beautiful, and we've had so much fun here. But I miss sleeping in my bed, playing in our garden, and seeing our friends," Millie explained. "Mom and Dad said that we can always come back here. So, if we leave now, we'll feel more excited to come back next time."

"Okay. Still, I feel kind of sad that we're leaving," Noah admitted.

"Then let's make this the best last day ever," Millie said.

Millie wanted to revisit some of the places where they'd had the most fun together as a family. Dad said that they could go, but only if Grandpa went with them.

First, Millie wanted to walk along the trail again, and she smiled when she saw Katherine, a young girl who lived in the National Park. Her parents took care of the hotel at the park, and they lived in a small house next to the hotel.

Katherine was about 12 years old, and they'd met on the second day of the holiday.

"Hi!" Katherine said as she ran toward Noah and Millie.

"Hi, Katherine!" Millie said.

"Hi! What are you doing here?" asked Noah.

"I'm out on my usual morning walk," answered the little girl. "How about you? Why are you walking around so early in the morning?"

"It's our last day here," Noah said with a sigh.

"Noah's feeling a bit sad," Millie explained.

"Oh, I see," Katherine said. "I understand why you feel sad, Noah. But if you keep the memories you have in your mind and heart, you can always keep coming back here."

"That's a nice way to put it," Noah said.

"I agree. And if we make this day the best one, we can bring home even more amazing memories with us!" Millie exclaimed.

Grandpa asked Katherine to join them, and happily Katherine said "Come with me, I want to show you something super cool."

Katherine led them all along the trail. After some time, she turned right.

"Wait, there is no trail there," Millie said.

"Yes. But don't worry about it. I always explore this part of the park," Katherine assured them.

They walked through some trees, then started climbing upward. They kept walking until Katherine stopped. She turned around to her new friends and grinned.

"Here we are," she said.

Noah, Millie and Grandpa walked up to where Katherine was standing. They discovered that they were in a clearing. Millie gasped and Noah's eyes grew wide as they saw the beautiful view through the trees.

"That's amazing!" Millie exclaimed, grasping Grandpa's hand.

"It's so beautiful," Noah whispered.

"I know! This is my favorite spot because I can see the whole park from here. I come here when I want to think or be by myself," Katherine said.

The three children sat down in a circle, and Grandpa sat on a log nearby smiling at them. Since Katherine had shared her favorite spot with them, Noah and Millie wanted to share their favorite memories with her.

"My favorite is when we explored the hidden trail and saw different animals," Noah said.

"For me, it was the time we made music together using different things that we found in nature," Millie said.

They talked and talked for what seemed like hours. Katherine told stories about how amazing it was to live in the National Park while Noah and Millie shared stories about how cool it was living in their neighborhood.

When it was time for them to go, they all thanked Katherine for being so kind. They went back to their hotel where Mom and Dad were waiting. That afternoon, as they drove home, the two children felt thankful for everything they experienced at the park.

And they looked forward to the time when they would be back to see their new friend and spend time in the beautiful National Park.

ONTO THE NEXT ADVENTURE...

Have you ever been to a place where you enjoyed the beauty of nature too?

Noah and Millie love the great outdoors and they were able to spend a week in a place where they made wonderful memories together. The best part was that they were able to spend quality time with their parents, grandparents, and with each other. But now, back home, it's time for you to hear more stories.

Hearing the next stories about Noah and Millie will surely help you feel happy and confident...

Chapter 7

The Power of Confidence and Acceptance

THE BOLD PERFORMER

N oah and Millie were two bright and talented children. They grew up with love and support from Mom and Dad, and they felt secure and loved. This gave them a sense of confidence, so they were always ready and happy to try new things when asked.

One morning, at school, Noah's teacher Ms. Jillian shared some exciting news with them. She said, "A few weeks ago, we had a Family Talent Show. All of the teachers and staff here at school loved everyone's performance. We all loved your performances so much that we decided to have a Talent Competition."

"Wow!" Noah exclaimed.

"Anyone can join the competition and I would encourage you all to join so that you can share your talents once more. And this time, we have some lovely trophies for the children who will win," explained Ms. Jillian.

Right away, Noah knew that he would join. He had a lot of fun during the Family Talent Show, and he wanted to share his talent again. The little boy played the guitar well, and he was already thinking about which song he would play.

When the recess bell rang, Noah rushed to Millie's classroom. He arrived there just as his big sister walked out of her classroom.

"Hi, Noah! What are you doing here?"

"Did Ms. Jen tell you about the Talent Competition?" he asked with a grin. Ms. Jen was Millie's teacher.

"Yes, she did," Millie answered.

"I'm still thinking about what song I will play on my guitar. Have you decided what song you will sing?" Noah asked.

"Oh, I won't be joining the Talent Competition. Our grade will have a Science Fair on the same day and Ms. Jen picked me to participate in the Science Fair. I asked her if I could join both competitions, but she said that I couldn't," Millie explained.

"Oh, that's too bad," Noah said.

"You're an amazing guitar player!" Millie exclaimed. "And to make it more fun, you should encourage your friends to join as well. That way, you can all practice together."

"That's a great idea," Noah said.

The little boy thanked his sister, then went back to his classroom. Once there, Noah saw that his friends were gathered in the middle of the room.

"What's going on?" Noah asked.

"We're talking about who will join the Talent Competition," answered Shawn, one of Noah's classmates.

"That's great!" Noah exclaimed. "I'm joining the competition, so who's with me?"

Sadly, nobody answered him. They all looked quite nervous even though Noah knew that his classmates were very talented too.

"Come on! We all had fun during the Family Talent Show, right? We can do that again. And we can even make it more fun by practicing together," Noah said with a smile.

Still, nobody said anything. That is until Shawn said, "I did have a lot of fun when I performed with my parents..."

"I did too," admitted Wendy, another one of their classmates. "But I performed with my mom, not by myself. I don't think that I can get up on stage on my own."

Noah was surprised when his other classmates agreed with her.

"So... you're all unsure because you don't feel confident enough?" Noah wondered.

One by one, Noah's classmates nodded. The little boy understood how they felt, and he wanted to help them feel better.

"Why don't we do this? We can all practice together so that we can share our talents with each other. Then we can take turns performing in front of everyone," Noah suggested. "Would that make it easier for you to get used to performing in front of others?"

"That's a good idea," Wendy said. "I can practice my dance, and when I'm good enough, I can dance in front of all of you."

"That's right. You will be able to see how it feels to perform in front of others before getting up on stage," Noah said.

"It's worth a try," said Shawn and everyone else agreed.

Noah felt happy! For the next few days, the little boy practiced his talent with his friends. They all enjoyed practicing together, and they all encouraged each other. Noah and his friends learned how to accept and appreciate each other much more.

Their friendship also grew stronger as the day of the Talent Competition arrived.

Thanks to Noah, all the children in his class were able to share their unique talents, singing, dancing, playing the flute, and playing the guitar like Noah. They were no longer nervous and shy, and they all shone brightly along with Noah in their own unique way.

THE BRAVE EXPLORERS

Noah and Millie were brave and adventurous children, full of imagination and ideas. They were very creative and had amazing adventures together, no matter where they were.

One morning, after eating breakfast, the two children went into their backyard. They didn't have school because it was the weekend, and they were trying to decide what they could do for the day.

"I wish we could go to the park," Noah said.

"Me too. But Mom and Dad said that they needed us to stay home today. So, we have to make the most of it," Millie said.

"Do you want to play catch?" suggested the little boy.

"Hmmm," Millie said. "How about something more exciting?"

"Like what?" Noah wondered.

"Well, we are out here in our backyard, one of our favorite places for an adventure," Millie said. She walked over to the tree where Dad built them a small tree house. The little girl looked for the rope that they used to climb up to the tree house.

After untying the rope, Millie grinned at her brother and said, "It's time for us to begin another adventure, Noah."

"Yes!" cried Noah excitedly.

Millie climbed up the rope and called Noah to join her. When they were both at the top, they opened the door to the tree house and stepped inside.

"I think we've found an abandoned house," Millie whispered.

Right away, the little boy knew that their adventure had really begun. He looked around excitedly and asked, "Do you have any idea who used to live here?"

"If you look at everything in this little house, you'll notice something. The person who lived here must have loved traveling.

There are maps and drawings of fantastic places, like desert islands and pirate caves with maps of buried treasure. There is even a backpack with a water bottle. Maybe the person who lived here was an explorer," Millie said.

In fact, everything in the tree house belonged to Noah and Millie. It had been a while since they'd played in there, which is why there were spider webs, and it was so dusty inside. But the last time they did play there, Noah and Millie had used the colored pens and drawing paper Grandma had given them.

And the backpack with the water bottle belonged to Dad because he had played with them the last time they visited the tree house.

"But... What happened to the explorer who lived here?" Noah asked wide-eyed.

"That's what we have to find out. Look at the floor, there are muddy footprints leading to the window. Maybe something was chasing him, and he had to escape!" Millie exclaimed.

"We should follow the footprints!" Noah said excitedly.

So, the two children went to work. They followed the muddy footprints that led to the window, then they squeezed through the window. Then Noah grabbed the rope and climbed down with Millie following him a few moments later.

Once they were on the ground, Millie said, "Oh, no. There are no more footprints to follow."

"That's okay. We just need to find more clues," Noah assured his sister.

To find those clues, they explored the backyard, which had been transformed into a jungle in their minds. They jumped across wild rivers, tried to cross crumbling bridges, and even entered dark caves.

Each time they found a clue, like an old watch, a pair of dirty socks, and a baseball cap, the two children felt delighted. They placed all of the clues they found in a bag that Noah took from their house.

Just when they were about to go back to the tree house to take a closer look at their clues, a beautiful woman walked into the jungle.

"There you are!" she said.

Noah and Millie were surprised! The little girl asked, "Do you know us?"

"Of course!" answered the beautiful woman, smiling.

"How can you know us when we've only just arrived in this jungle?" Noah wondered.

"Ah," said the beautiful woman. "I must have been mistaken. I am looking for my two precious children as they need to come back inside the house for a while."

Right away, the jungle that Noah and Millie imagined changed back into their backyard.

"Hi, Mom!" said Noah, as he gave her a hug.

"Reporting for duty!" Millie said with a giggle.

"It seems like you were having a lot of fun," Mom said.

"We pretended to be explorers looking for someone in a jungle," Millie explained.

"What fun!" Mom said cheerfully. "You were brave to be all alone in a jungle!"

Noah handed his bag to Mom and said, "While exploring, we found these. I think this old watch and dirty socks are Dad's."

They all had a good laugh, then Mom knelt down and looking at Millie and Noah said, "You've had quite an adventure. Being explorers can be hard, but I know that you are brave enough to face any challenge and keep going no matter how difficult things can get!"

THE UNIQUE PUZZLE PIECE

Noah and Millie loved their town, their neighborhood, their school, and the park. For them, it was the best place to live.

One morning, Dad said to Noah "Would you like to come and help me run some errands in town? Mom has asked Millie to help her clean the attic, so it's just you and me!"

"I'd love to!" Noah said excitedly. "I'll tell Millie all about it when we get home."

So, Dad and Noah left to run some errands. Even though they lived in a small town, they had to ride in Dad's car because they had a lot of places to go to, including the supermarket and Mom's shopping list was very long.

Their first stop was the hardware store where Dad had to buy some tools for his project back home. He was making a small bathroom cabinet and he needed to buy some nails, screws, and a new hammer.

While on their way to the store Dad said, "You know Noah, our town is like a big jigsaw puzzle."

"What do you mean, Dad?" asked Noah.

"Each part of the town is like a piece of a giant puzzle, and when all those parts are put together, they form this town that we all love. Even the people make up parts of the puzzle." Dad said.

"That's a really nice way to think about our town," Noah said with a smile.

"I just thought about it," said Dad, "because I saw you and Millie doing your puzzle on the floor yesterday. The one of the farm with all the animals."

Noah smiled. He and Millie had really enjoyed putting the pieces together to make the whole picture of the farm. When they reached the hardware store, Dad parked the car.

"Let's go!" Dad said. "We need to get a lot of things, and you can help me find them. But stay close to me, okay? It's easy to get lost in all these aisles. Who knows who we'll meet?"

They got a cart to put all the items in, and Noah helped to push it. While walking around, Dad met a lot of people he knew in the store.

First, he met a big man wearing a bright yellow jacket.

The man said, "It's nice to see you here, and who's this young man?"

"It's nice to see you too, Bill. This is my son, Noah," Dad said.

"Hello," said the little boy.

With a friendly smile, Bill held out his hand to shake Noah's and said, "Hello Noah. I'm Bill, and I'm a firefighter. Tell your Dad to bring you to see me at the fire station, so I can show you around sometime."

Wow! Noah was so excited! Firefighters were his heroes. He waved to Bill as the big man walked away.

In the next aisle, Noah saw his teacher, Ms. Jillian. She was happy to see him and Dad and told them she was getting colored string for a school project.

"I'll tell you about it tomorrow in class," she said and waved goodbye.

The next person they saw was the town vet. His name was Dr. Ray, and he always took very good care of Whiskers whenever the little cat got sick. Noah and Millie liked him a lot because he loved animals so much.

As Dad and Noah walked to the cashier desk, they ran into Miguel, the town plumber. Miguel was very good at his job and used a lot of strange-looking tools. He always greeted Noah and Millie with a high-five whenever he saw them.

As they walked back to the car, Dad said they had to go to the dentist to make an appointment for the family, and then collect a package for Grandma at the Post Office. Their last stop was at the supermarket, where they got all the things on Mom's long shopping list.

Eventually, it was time to get in the car and travel home. Noah was feeling very happy.

"Thank you so much Noah for all your help today," Dad said. "We had fun going to so many places in our giant jigsaw town, didn't we?"

Noah smiled. His Dad was right. Each place they'd been to was a piece of the puzzle. Even the different people they met were like unique pieces of the puzzle.

Noah felt happy and proud to live in such a town and couldn't wait to tell Millie about his morning out with Dad.

THE CONFIDENT LEADER

Noah and Millie were two very confident children, and they never shied away from doing anything new.

One morning, Mom and Dad had to drop them off at school earlier than usual, because they had a meeting to go to. Noah went to the playground while Millie went straight to her class.

Mom had bought Millie a new book, and she wanted to start reading it while waiting for her classmates to arrive. Millie soon got lost in the adventures about a family of bears. She was so focused on her book that she didn't hear Ms. Jen come in.

"Good morning, Millie! It's nice to see you here so early," said Ms. Jen.

Millie looked up in surprise and smiled. She then explained why she was in the class so early.

"Well, I am extra happy to see you here because I wanted to talk to you about something," Ms. Jen said.

The little girl put her book mark in the middle of the pages she was reading.

"I was so impressed with your project at the Science Fair two weeks ago and all the other teachers were too," Ms. Jen said.

"Thank you," said Millie, blushing a little.

"Since we're nearing the end of the school year," said Ms. Jen, "Each class must work together to create a group project. We will present it in a program in the main Assembly Hall on the last day of school."

"That sounds wonderful!" Millie exclaimed.

"You can share any ideas you have along with your classmates," said her teacher. "But I wanted to talk to you about being the leader of this project. I think you would be just right for the job, since all your classmates look up to you."

"Really? Thank you, I'll be happy to work with my friends. It'll be fun. We'll do our best to make it the best project ever!" said the little girl confidently.

Millie's classmates came into the room and their teacher told them about the project.

"I have decided to assign Millie to be your project leader, so I hope that you all listen to her and work well together," Ms. Jen requested.

Everyone cheered for Millie. They were all excited and Ms. Jen gave them time to share their ideas and plan their project.

Millie stood up in front of the class and called one of her classmates to the front too. She said, "Laura will write down all of our ideas, then we'll vote on which one we will use. I know you all have great ideas, so let's start sharing!"

The kids were eager to share their ideas. Millie smiled as everyone worked well together and their teacher was impressed by Millie as she encouraged all her friends.

"These are really good!" Millie exclaimed after everyone had shared their ideas. "Now, let's vote."

After the first vote, the shortlist of ideas was:

1. Keeping a pet

2. Friendship

3. Musical instruments

In the end, the kids chose "Friendship" as their class project. They had all spent a year in the same class, got to know each other well, and had become good friends.

"Thank you, Millie. And thank you, everyone. I'm very proud of how well you work together," said Ms. Jen, with tears in her eyes. She really loved the kids in her class, and she would miss them when school was over.

Millie, as leader, encouraged her classmates to create the best project the school had ever seen. Together they made a giant poster with the word FRIENDSHIP in brightly colored letters. They even wrote a poem and chose a song about friendship to sing in front of the whole school.

Millie presented the project on the last day of school while her little brother Noah was sitting in the big hall. He cheered for Millie as she got up onto the stage.

When the principal asked Millie how they had created such an amazing piece of work, Millie smiled at him and at her classmates and said, "It's all about teamwork!"

ONTO THE NEXT ADVENTURE...

Do you feel as brave and confident as Noah and Millie?

These two siblings have always shown the world that they believed in themselves, and they weren't afraid to face challenges. These are important lessons that all children need to learn. Even you can be confident if you start believing in yourself just like the two children.

Now it's time to embark on incredible quests filled with wonder through the stories in the next chapter...

Chapter 8

Noah and Millie's Quest for Wonder

THE SPACE EXPLORERS

N oah and Millie loved to learn new things at school, and then share what they learned with the family at teatime and at weekends.

One afternoon, the two children hung out in their backyard. It was one of their favorite places in the world because they had lots of adventures there.

"What did you learn in school this week?" Millie asked her brother.

"Oh! This week was super fun as Ms. Jillian taught us all about the solar system," Noah said excitedly.

"No way! That's what we are doing in class too!" Millie exclaimed.

The two children talked about the planets, the stars, and the whole universe. Even though they both learned about the solar system, their teachers had taught them different things.

Noah's class learned the names of the different planets and how they were arranged in the solar system. Being a bright little boy, Noah memorized the names of the planets in order right away.

Millie's teacher taught her and her friends interesting facts in more detail about the planets.

"That's so cool! I would love to learn more about the different planets too," Noah said.

"I'd love to teach you! But... would you like to make our lesson more exciting?" Millie asked mysteriously.

"Of course!" Noah replied.

"Great! Wait here," she said, then she ran inside the house.

Moments later, Millie came back outside. Noah was surprised to see Mom and Dad following her. They were carrying a bunch of stuff.

"What's all this?" Noah wondered.

"Millie said that you will be learning about space. So, we decided to help," Dad explained.

The two children watched as Mom and Dad pitched a tent for them in the backyard. Then Dad set up a telescope for them to use.

"The sun has started to set," Mom said. "It's the perfect time to learn about the stars, the planets, and everything else in the solar system."

"This is great! Thanks, Mom and Dad," said Millie with a smile. Then she turned to Noah, "I just asked them if we can do a stargazing activity after dinner, but they had a better idea."

"This is awesome! Thanks, Mom. Thanks, Dad," Noah said.

"Now, you're all set," Dad said.

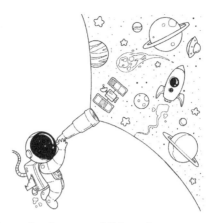

Mom and Dad taught the two children how to use the telescope. Before going back to the house, Mom said, "Since it is too bright, you can't see the stars in the sky yet. For now, while you wait for the sun to go down, you can both sit in the tent and Millie can teach you all about the planets."

"That's not just a tent, Mom," Millie said. "It's a ship for space explorers!"

"How cool!" Dad exclaimed.

"Well then, have fun!" said Mom, smiling, as she walked back into the house with Dad.

The two children went inside their pretend spaceship and sat down. It was super comfortable because Mom had filled it with soft pillows. Once inside, Millie zipped the door shut. Then she sat next to the window with Noah.

They pretended to take off in their ship and fly into space. As Noah named the planets that whizzed by, Millie shared some interesting facts about those planets.

"Look, it's Venus!" Noah exclaimed.

"Venus is known as Earth's twin and it's filled with foul-smelling gas," Millie explained, holding her nose as Noah giggled.

"How about Mars?" Noah asked. "It's that planet over there."

"Mars is known as the red planet," Millie explained. "It's very hot there because it's so close to the sun."

Noah continued to name the planets while Millie shared what she knew. Soon, the sun had set, and it was already dark.

"I guess it's time for us to land," said Millie.

After they landed safely in their backyard, Noah opened the tent door. The two children stepped out excitedly and ran to the telescope.

"You can go first," Millie said to her brother.

"Thanks!" Noah exclaimed before peeking through the telescope.

"Wow! You can really see the stars from here!" exclaimed the little boy. "They look so close!" Then he moved the telescope gently to see more of the night sky. "I think I see Venus!"

Millie waited patiently for her brother to finish. While waiting, she smiled as the little boy named everything that he spotted. Moments later, Mom and Dad came out of the house. Mom had a tray with burgers, a pitcher of juice, and some glasses.

"Are you having fun?" Dad asked.

"Yes!" cried the two children happily.

The night continued on as the whole family enjoyed their dinner. Mom and Dad answered all of the kid's questions about space, and Noah and Millie had so much fun learning that they promised to never get tired of discovering new things!

THE AMAZING MUSEUM

Noah and Millie enjoyed exploring their town. Whenever their parents invited them to go into town, they always agreed.

So, when Grandma and Grandpa invited the two children to go to the museum in town at the weekend, they were both very excited!

"I've never been to the museum before!" cried Noah.

"I think I've gone there once, but I don't really remember," Millie said.

"You're right, Millie. Grandma and I took you and your parents to the museum when it opened years ago. You were still a baby then, so I'm not surprised that you don't remember," Grandpa explained.

The two children got dressed and waited for their grandparents in the garden. Soon, they saw Grandpa's red car driving down the road.

"Here they come!" Noah exclaimed.

Millie ran into the house to tell their parents that Grandma and Grandpa were close. Moments later, she came back outside with Mom and Dad.

"Come on in!" Grandpa said cheerfully as he stopped the car right next to the gate.

Noah and Millie hugged their parents, then hopped into Grandpa's car.

"We're ready!" Millie said excitedly.

"Then let's go," said Grandma.

The museum wasn't very far from Noah and Millie's house, so they arrived in just a few minutes. After parking the car, Grandpa, Grandma and the two children walked toward the museum.

Before going inside, Grandma knelt down in front of the children. She said, "The museum contains many precious objects. So, you shouldn't touch anything. Also, the people who come here want to learn and appreciate the things inside the museum. So, when we're there, try not to make too much noise."

The two children nodded, and they all went inside.

Millie gasped as she saw rows and rows of glass cases inside the museum.

In a soft voice, Grandpa said, "Everything you will find here are from different cultures and time periods in history. Look at these. What do you think they are?"

Noah and Millie stared at the objects inside the glass case at which Grandpa was pointing.

"They look like bowls, but they're very old and dirty. I thought that the items in museums were valuable," Noah observed.

"That's exactly right, Noah. These are bowls found in caves back when people used to live in caves instead of houses. The ones we have now are usually made of china or plastic, but these bowls here were made of clay," Grandpa explained.

"They might look dirty and old, but they tell us a lot about how people used to live in the past," said Grandma. "So, they are really special and precious."

"Wow," Millie said. "So, the people who found these bowls were able to find out more about the lives of people who lived in caves because of these simple items?"

"Yes," said Grandpa with a smile. "Everything we see here helps us to have a better picture of how life started out in a simple way and gradually changed into what it is now."

"That's so awesome. I can't wait to see more," Noah said with a grin.

So, the two children and their grandparents continued around the museum. The two children were amazed as they saw suits of armor, simple tools, masks, jewelry, and more. There were even strange-looking objects that Grandpa and Grandma couldn't name.

Then they entered another room that was filled with statues of men, women, and children. They were wearing costumes from different countries and time periods. Millie loved this part of the museum because they were so colorful, and she imagined dressing up in them.

"When I get home, I'll try to draw these beautiful costumes in my sketchbook," she said.

"Grandma, can we have another painting activity in your house soon? I'd love to paint some of the amazing things we've seen today!" Noah asked.

"Of course, we can, Noah," Grandma replied, giving him a hug.

With each room that they entered, the two children felt even more excited. By the time they reached the end of their tour, they couldn't stop talking about everything they'd seen!

"Thank you for bringing us to the museum," Millie said with a smile.

"You're welcome," said Grandma. "I'm so glad that you enjoyed yourselves. It's important to learn about different cultures and history, and learning through discovery and exploration is the best way to do this. You can read about them in a book, but it's much more realistic and fun when you see them in a museum, isn't it?"

You could see from Noah and Millie's smiling faces that they agreed.

That evening, sitting up in bed in their pajamas, they were still telling Mom and Dad about their outing with Grandpa and Grandma to the museum. They would always remember what they saw and would no doubt sleep very well that night.

THE TIME TRAVELERS

Noah and Millie had just discovered the wonders of learning about the past. They recently visited a museum with their grandparents, where they discovered fascinating things that made them want to learn even more.

One morning, the two children decided to play with their friends at the park. Once there, they all sat in a circle to decide what they were going to do.

"I say we chase each other around the park," said Jared, one of Noah and Millie's friends.

"We always play chasing games," Grace said grumpily. "I want to play something more fun."

"How about... hide-and-seek?" suggested Nina.

"The park is too big for us to play hide-and-seek. It might take us forever to find each other," said Chuck with a laugh.

"We have an idea," Noah said with a grin. "And we're sure you'll all love it!"

"Really? What is it?" asked Grace.

"Well Noah and I visited the museum with our grandparents last week and it was super cool," Millie explained. "So why don't we pretend like we're time travelers going on an adventure?"

"That sounds awesome!" exclaimed Justin.

"Then let's go!" said Noah cheerfully.

Millie led the group of children to the jungle gym. They all crawled under the jungle gym and pretended like it was their very own time machine.

"Before we go, we have some rules," Noah announced. "Going to the past is fun, but you shouldn't touch anything! Changing something in the past might have a great effect on our world now."

"Wow. Where did you learn that?" Millie wondered.

"I saw it in a movie once," answered the little boy with a grin.

"Are we all ready?" Millie asked.

"Yes!" cried everyone excitedly.

"Let's go!" Millie exclaimed.

First, the children went way back into the past, to a time when people used to live in caves. Noah and Millie explained how people used bowls and plates made of clay to place their food in.

"Since they didn't have machines to make anything in plastic, they made their own bowls out of clay. Imagine how difficult that would be to do today!" Noah said with wide eyes.

"I couldn't make my own bowls or plates," Grace admitted. "I'm not very artistic."

Next, the children went to a time when people used to wear robes and simple clothes.

"Do you mean that even little girls couldn't wear pretty dresses or shorts with frills on them?" asked Nina with wide eyes as the little girl loved to dress up in fancy clothes.

"Back then, they didn't have clothes like those. They all dressed simply," Millie said.

"I wouldn't want to live in that time," said Nina, which made Millie smile.

The next time period they visited was more familiar to them because the houses had electricity instead of candles. Noah told his friends that they were getting closer to their own time.

"Still, there were no computers, tablets, and smartphones yet. There were no televisions either," he told them.

"No TVs or computers?" asked Jared with wide eyes. "So, what did they do all day and night?"

"They played together," said Millie with a giggle. "Playing is fun, right? It's what we're doing right now!"

"Well, I guess so," said Jared even though he didn't seem too sure.

The two children continued to take their friends on an imaginative exploration of different times in history. Noah and Millie shared everything they had learned from the museum visit with their grandparents.

And with each trip, they got closer to the present. When their journey in the time machine was over, the two children were happy to see how excited their friends were.

"I can't believe life has changed so much!" exclaimed Nina.

"Can you imagine living in a cave?" Grace asked her friends. "It must have been so cold there whenever winter came along!"

"After learning about life in the past, I really appreciate everything we have now. I feel like life is a lot easier for us because of all the discoveries and inventions that people made in the past," Millie said.

"As for me, I feel bad for the children of the past. I don't think they had as much fun as we have now," Noah shared.

"Well, we don't know that for sure," Millie said. "What we do know is that everything we have now has come from smart, hardworking people who wanted to change our lives for the better."

"Thank you both for sharing so much about the past," Jared said, and the other kids agreed. Jared continued, "Those are lessons we will surely remember for a long, long time. Let's do something like this again soon."

They all returned to their homes, happy and so glad to have friends like Millie and Noah.

ONTO THE NEXT ADVENTURE...

Do you enjoy learning new things through discovery and exploration too?

Noah and Millie love discovering new things and to make learning even more fun, they do this in different ways. In these stories, they visited Outer Space, went to a museum, and even traveled back in time! What exciting ways to discover more about the world!

With so many good things around them, it's time to hear stories about being grateful...

Chapter 9

The Power of Gratitude

THE KINDNESS JARS

Noah and Millie were blessed with a happy family, and they felt so loved that they wanted to do something special for all the people closest to them.

"What can we do, Millie? We can't buy gifts for everyone. Even if we saved up a lot of money in our piggy banks, I don't think there's enough there to buy everyone a present," Noah said to his sister one afternoon.

The two children were sitting in their living room. Millie sighed. Noah was right, of course. Still, they wanted to do something to show the people they loved how thankful they were for having them in their lives.

The little girl tried to think of other ideas, but nothing came to her mind!

Just then, Grandma came into the living room. She was carrying a tray filled with their favorite snack, cookies and milk.

"Did you bake those cookies, Grandma?" Noah asked excitedly.

"Yes, I did. But they aren't freshly baked. I made these last night since I knew that I was coming over here today," Grandma explained.

"That's okay! Any cookies baked by you are the best cookies in the universe!" exclaimed the little boy as he hugged his grandma.

Then he helped Grandma place the tray on the table before taking one of the cookies, the biggest chocolate chip one he could find.

"Why do you look so worried, Millie? Is everything okay?" Grandma wondered as she sat next to the little girl, putting her arms around her.

Millie told Grandma what she and Noah wanted to do. Then she said, "Noah and I have been thinking of ways to show how thankful we are, but we can't think of anything!"

"Oh, I have the perfect suggestion. It's something I did many moons ago when I was young. Would you like to hear it?" Grandma suggested.

"Of course!" Millie said cheerfully.

Before sharing her idea, Grandma asked the two children to gather some items from the house. She asked them to find two empty jars with lids, sheets of colored paper, two pairs of scissors, markers, and an empty box.

When the children had gathered everything, Grandma said, "Let's make some Kindness Jars. Each day, you will write three things that you feel thankful about. Three nice things that your friends or family have done for you along with words of thanks and appreciation.

"Then you can roll up those colored pieces of paper notes and place them in your jars. Do this every day until your jars are full. Once you've filled your jars, you can give the little notes to your loved ones!"

"Wow, that's such an amazing idea, Grandma!" Millie exclaimed with wide eyes.

"Can we start now?" Noah asked.

"That's why I asked you to bring all of these items," Grandma said with a smile. "First, we need to cut these sheets of colored paper into small pieces."

The two children cut the paper into different shapes, some round, some square. When they were done, they placed the small pieces of paper in the empty box. Then Noah and Millie took three pieces of paper each and started writing.

While they wrote on their sheets of paper, Grandma used the markers to write the names of the children on each of the jars.

"How lovely!" Millie said happily after Grandma showed them the two jars with their names. The little girl thanked her grandma as she took the jar with her name. In exchange, she handed a pink note to Grandma.

"I know that I'm just getting started, but I wanted you to have this, Grandma," Millie said.

"Hey! That's what I thought too!" Noah exclaimed as he waved a small blue note in the air. He also handed his note to his grandma.

"How sweet!" Grandma exclaimed. She read their notes out loud, "You are the best grandma in the world, and you bake the yummiest cookies! Oh, thank you, Noah! I think you're the best grandson in the world."

Noah jumped up and hugged her. Then Grandma read Millie's note, "Thank you for showing us how to make Kindness Jars. You're the best grandma ever!"

"What a coincidence! You're the best granddaughter ever, too!" said Grandma.

Millie jumped up and hugged Grandma just like Noah did. Now that their Kindness Jars were ready, they kept both jars and the box with small sheets of paper on a table in their bedroom.

Every day after school, they wrote three notes for the people they loved, rolled the notes up, and placed them in the jars. A few weeks later their jars were filled. One afternoon, the two children took out the notes and gave them to Mom, Dad, and their grandparents. Then they went to the park and gave the notes to their special friends there who they always played with.

They felt good about telling everyone how thankful they were. In turn, the special people who received their notes felt happy and loved too.

A BLESSING IN DISGUISE

Noah and Millie were always thrilled to go on field trips because they loved exploring new places! Whenever they heard about a new trip planned by their teachers, they would be overjoyed. Then they would spend a lot of time wondering what activities they would do on the trip.

Two weeks ago, their teachers told them about the field trip to the zoo. Noah and Millie felt so excited that they couldn't think of anything else. Now that their trip was just a few days away, the two children were over the moon!

But the weekend came, along with bad weather. When they woke up, both children felt sad. They wanted to play outside, but they couldn't because of the rain.

After breakfast, Millie asked Noah if he wanted to play board games, but the little boy only shook his head and said, "I wanted to play outside."

"We can't do that because of the rain," Millie said. "But we still have our field trip to look forward to, right?"

That made Noah smile. He stood up and agreed to play board games with his big sister.

The weekend passed by quickly and by Sunday night, the two children were too excited to sleep. The rain stopped that afternoon and they both looked forward to a sunny morning.

Sadly, when they woke up the next day, it was raining again.

"Oh, no," said Noah. "Do you think we can still go to the zoo today?"

"Let's ask Mom," suggested Millie.

The two children, still in their pajamas, ran to the dining room to look for Mom. When they got there, Mom had just said goodbye to someone on the phone, then she sighed. She looked quite sad when she saw the two children standing by the doorway.

"I'm so sorry, but that was Ms. Jillian. Your field trip to the zoo has been canceled because of the rain," she said.

Tears formed in Noah's eyes while Millie tried to fight back her own tears. She didn't want to cry because she knew that it would make her little brother cry even more.

Instead, the little girl asked, "So, do we stay home today?"

"I'm afraid so. Now, why don't you two change out of your pajamas and I'll prepare an extra special meal for you," Mom suggested gently.

"That's okay, Mom. Extra special breakfasts are for days when we go to the zoo," Noah said sadly as he walked out of the dining room. Millie sighed, then followed her brother.

The two children sat on their beds without saying a word to each other. They both felt sad and disappointed. They didn't even feel hungry. Neither of them wanted to do anything but sit on their beds.

Then, out of nowhere came a loud trumpeting sound that made the two children jump!

"What was that?" Noah cried.

Before Millie could answer, their door flung open and in came Dad wearing an elephant costume! He blew the trumpet again and laughed aloud.

Noah and Millie were giggling when Mom came into the room too. She was dressed like a zookeeper.

With a big grin, she said, "Are you two ready for your zoo adventure?"

The two children looked at each other and grinned. Then they jumped off their beds and said, "Yes!"

Noah and Millie followed their parents into the living room. Their eyes grew wide when they saw how their parents had transformed their living room into a zoo! Their stuffed animals were scattered all around the room and in the middle of the table was an art center where they could draw different kinds of animals.

Mom also piled all of their animal-printed clothes and costumes on one of the chairs.

"Before we start our tour, go ahead and change into your favorite animal clothing!" Mom exclaimed.

Noah wore his favorite tiger hoodie while Millie wore her dress that had colorful parrots on it. Then they joined their parents on a tour of their zoo at home. Noah and Millie had tons of fun as they visited different animals in the zoo and listened to fun facts about each one.

Then they drew their favorite animals using the art materials on the table.

While they were drawing, Mom produced their favorite drinks and sandwiches she'd made, and said, "Are you having fun?"

"Yes!" exclaimed Millie.

Noah nodded because he'd just taken a big bite of his sandwich.

"Then I guess the rain was a blessing in disguise," Dad said. "Even if you weren't able to go to the zoo, you were still able to have fun with animals. You see, when a challenge comes your way, you can either give up or find a way to make things better."

"Now, let's take a photo together to remember this amazing day," Mom said. "Would you like to change your clothes again?"

Noah rummaged through the pile of clothes happily, until he found his favorite crocodile onesie, and Millie looked for her favorite animal t-shirt.

"Got it!" she exclaimed. It had a picture of a cuddly koala on the front.

"We're ready!" Noah said happily after they both got changed.

"So are we," Mom said.

To the delight of the children, Mom and Dad changed their clothes too. Dad wore a lion costume while Mom wore a beautiful blue dress with a picture of a swan on it.

"Let's all sit on the sofa," Mom said.

While Dad, Noah and Millie sat down on the couch, Mom set up the camera, and after taking some photos, the family continued playing their zoo games until bedtime.

They'd had a wonderful day and that night they fell asleep happily.

The Appreciation Picnic

Noah and Millie loved their family very much. They knew how to appreciate others, which was something they learned from Mom, Dad, Grandpa, and Grandma.

The two children often spent time in their backyard, playing, sharing stories, or using their imaginations to go on adventures. One morning, after having a fun adventure, they sat on the grass in the sunshine.

"Tomorrow is Sunday. What do you want to do?" Noah asked.

"I was thinking of doing something special for Mom, Dad, Grandma, and Grandpa," the little girl answered. "They do so many things for us, and I want to show them how thankful we are."

"That's a nice idea," Noah agreed. "But what can we do?"

"How about having an Appreciation Picnic for them?" Millie suggested.

"What's that?" Noah wondered.

It's a special picnic where we prepare everything, like the food and games, and we can get colored balloons too!" Millie said.

"Sounds great! We can play their favorite picnic games," Noah said.

"That's perfect! Now, all we have to do is prepare the food. But we have to do it in secret so that we can surprise them all," Millie said.

So, the two children got to work. Noah distracted Mom and Dad by asking them to help him look for something, which he had hidden on purpose. While their parents were busy, Millie rummaged through the kitchen to look for food.

She filled their picnic basket with fresh fruits, cold cuts, bread, and a container filled with potato salad that Mom made for Grandpa and Grandma. After filling the basket, she hid it in her room.

Then she took the object that Noah pretended to be looking for and went to find the rest of her family.

"Noah, is this what you were looking for?" she asked with a smile.

"There it is!" exclaimed the little boy. Then he turned to his parents and thanked them for helping him.

"Mom, Dad, can you please help me with my homework?" Millie asked, winking at Noah.

Mom and Dad went with her to her room. Noah went to the living room to make four invitations to the Appreciation Picnic for Mom, Dad, Grandpa and Grandma.

Noah worked hard on the invitations, and he tried to work quickly too. When he was done, he went to their room where he found Millie with Mom and Dad.

"Are you done?" Millie asked when she saw her brother.

Noah nodded, then handed one invitation each to Mom and Dad.

"What are these?" Dad asked.

Millie stood next to her little brother and said, "Noah and I have prepared a special picnic for you. We can have it in the backyard. But before we start, can we pick up Grandma and Grandpa too?"

"What a lovely idea!" Mom exclaimed.

"I can pick up Grandma and Grandpa," Dad offered.

"Thanks, Dad," said Millie as she handed her grandparents' invitations to him.

While Dad was gone, Mom and the two children went to the backyard to prepare for the picnic.

Once there, Noah said, "Just sit down and relax, Mom. We'll prepare everything."

Mom smiled as she sat down on the garden bench. Moments later, Millie brought her a glass of lemonade from the kitchen. Then the two children laid out the mat on the ground, and Millie brought the picnic basket that she'd kept hidden in their room.

Noah prepared a pitcher of lemonade and brought it outside as well. It was very heavy, so he walked slowly as he didn't want to spill any. Dad arrived with Grandma and Grandpa. The two children ran to hug their grandparents and welcome them to the Appreciation Picnic.

"Let's start by playing some games," Millie said with a grin. "The first is tug-of-war, Dad's favorite. Then we can play charades, which is Mom's favorite. After that, we can play a song guessing game for Grandma, and a relay race for Grandpa."

"Those are our favorite games!" Grandma said with delight.

After playing, they all sat down, tired but happy. Noah and Millie listened attentively while Mom, Dad, Grandma and Grandpa talked about when they were little children. They shared details about their family history which was fascinating for the two children, who asked lots of questions.

Before the picnic was over, Noah and Millie said a few words to show how much they loved and appreciated their family, then laughing out loud, they all got up and burst all the colored balloons.

ONTO THE NEXT ADVENTURE...

Do you thank the people in your life too?

Noah and Millie always made sure that the people they loved the most knew how thankful they were for everything they did. These stories were filled with love and kindness, two things that we all need in life. Hopefully, you felt inspired by these two children!

And now, for the last chapter, it's time to hear some stories about being amazingly fearless...

Chapter 10

The Fearless Ventures

FEARLESS MILLIE

N oah and Millie were confident children who were always willing to try new things. So, whenever someone asked them if they wanted to try something new, they both agreed right away.

That is, until one day, Mom asked Millie if she would like to take swimming lessons.

Ever since she could remember, Millie had been afraid of swimming. She enjoyed going to the beach, because she liked to play in the sand with Noah. She didn't mind playing by the shore either.

As long as the water didn't go up to her knees, she was okay.

But just the thought of jumping into the ocean or into a deep swimming pool made Millie go cold with fear.

"Millie? Are you alright?" Mom asked.

Mom told Millie that some very nice people were offering swimming lessons at school in Millie's grade, but, after hearing Mom's question, Millie's mind had gone blank.

"I'm sorry, but... I don't think I want to take swimming lessons, Mom," she admitted.

"Oh?" Mom asked. "Really? Come over here, what's wrong, Millie?"

It was the first time that Millie hadn't wanted to do something. Usually, she was always happy to try new things.

"I... I don't want to go swimming," Millie said again, lowering her head.

"Do you want to tell me why?" Mom asked gently as she didn't want the little girl to get upset.

"I'm afraid of drowning," Millie said softly. "I don't want to go where my feet can't touch the floor."

"I can understand that," said Mom. "To be honest, I prefer staying close to the shore, but I love swimming too. It's such fun when you know how."

"Really?" asked the little girl.

Mom then said, "Do you want to know a secret?"

"What?" Millie asked with wide eyes.

"Learning how to swim will help you face your fear," Mom said with a wink. "And you'll be a much happier girl for it."

"Oh...," said Millie.

"It's true!" Mom exclaimed. "Think about it, if you know how to swim, you'll be able to move around in the water whether you're in a swimming pool, at the beach, or even if you fall into a big vat of water!"

Millie giggled at the thought of falling into a big vat of water. She said, "Where would I ever find a vat of water big enough to fall in?"

"I don't know," Mom said as she started giggling too. "You and your brother are always going on adventures. If you know how to swim, then you won't have to worry even if you do fall into one!"

"That's silly, Mom!" Millie laughed.

But she did feel better. After discovering how learning how to swim could help her overcome fear of deep water, the little girl wondered if she was brave enough to try taking lessons.

"Will you come with me when I take swimming lessons?" Millie asked.

"Of course, Millie. I will be there to watch over you as long as you need me to be there," Mom assured her.

Finally, the little girl agreed.

Two days later, she went with Mom to their school to have her first swimming lesson.

"Good luck, Millie!" said Noah cheerfully before they left.

When they arrived at school, Millie saw that some of her friends from the class were there too. She felt a bit better after seeing them. Before allowing the children to get into the pool, the swimming teacher shared some rules for them to follow.

When the lesson started, Millie slowly got into the water. The teacher was so kind and showed Millie patiently and gently how to move in the water. Once she started following his advice, she discovered that swimming wasn't so bad after all.

In fact, she was even enjoying herself.

Soon, she had learned the proper way of moving her arms and feet. At the end of class, Millie felt tired, but very very happy.

She realized that her fear of swimming was just in her head. Mom was right. Learning how to swim made her feel confident, and she looked forward to her next lesson.

"You did so well!" Mom said happily after Millie got dressed.

"Thanks for encouraging me to take swimming lessons, Mom," said the little girl with a smile.

She felt like a superhero, brave and strong, and that night, as Mom tucked her into bed, she knew she'd have a very good night's sleep.

THE RESCUE MISSION

Noah and Millie were brave children who were always ready to lend a hand, as helping others made them feel good.

One afternoon, the two children were racing against each other in the backyard. They had to run all around the backyard three times, then try to find the flag that Dad had hidden somewhere in the area.

They were having so much fun until Millie stopped in her tracks. Noah turned to see if his sister was catching up to him. But she was just standing there with a strange look on her face.

The little boy walked up to his sister and asked, "Are you okay? Why did you stop running?"

"Shhh..." she said. "Listen."

Noah stood next to his sister and listened. Then his eyes grew wide as he heard something. It sounded like something was chirping somewhere in the bushes.

"Is that... a bird?" Noah wondered.

"It sounds like one. But why is it chirping so much? And why is the sound coming from the ground?" Millie asked.

"We should investigate," Noah suggested.

With a nod, Millie started walking and Noah followed her. The two children walked as quietly as possible so they could hear the sound they were trying to follow. The closer they got to the bushes, the louder the sound became.

"Look," Noah said while pointing to one of the bushes.

Millie saw that something was moving around behind the bush, which caused the branches and leaves to move around too. She knelt down in front of the bush and reached out.

"Wait! Are you sure that's safe?" Noah asked worriedly.

"It sounds like the bird is in trouble. If it is, we should help. Don't worry, I'll be careful," Millie assured her brother.

The little girl reached her hand into the bush and, very carefully, pushed the leaves and branches aside a little. Right away, the two children spotted the little bird that was making so much noise. It was a small yellow bird that was tangled in the bush.

The little bird chirped and chirped while trying to escape.

"The poor little thing is trapped," Millie said.

"What can we do? We can't just pull the little bird out of there. It looks like its feathers are tangled in the branches. It might get hurt," Noah said.

"You're right. We need to think of a plan to save the bird," Millie agreed. She moved her head closer to the bush and with a sweet soft voice, she said, "Don't worry, little one. We'll think of a way to help you, and we'll come straight back."

She gently let go of the branches and turned to her brother saying, "We need to work together."

"Do you have a plan?" Noah asked.

"Yes. We need a small pair of scissors and a pair of gloves. You get the scissors, and I'll ask Dad for our gloves, which should be somewhere in the garage," she said.

Noah went into their room to grab a pair of scissors from his school desk. Then he went back outside to wait for his sister.

Millie found Dad in the garage and said, "I'm just getting the gardening gloves Grandpa gave Noah and me last Spring."

"What are you two up to?" Dad asked, smiling.

Millie told him about the poor little yellow bird trapped in the bush. She also told him how they planned to save it. Dad handed her the gloves and said, "Be careful. Just call me if you need help."

Millie thanked him, then put on her gloves, and rejoined her brother.

She gave Noah his gloves and said, "I will hold the branches back and use the scissors to cut away everything that's trapping the bird. While I do that, I need you to hold the bird gently. Once it's free, let go so the bird can fly."

The two children got to work. Noah knelt down in front of the bird and gently held him in his hands and said with a soft voice, "Don't worry, I won't hurt you.

"Millie gave her brother a thumbs up, then she started cutting away the branches. Soon, the bird was free! Noah gently placed him on the ground. They watched the little bird stretch its wings and fly away.

"We did it!" Millie exclaimed.

Noah was happy too. By thinking of a plan quickly and working together, they found the courage to help the little bird that had been trapped in the bush, in the best and safest way possible. They both felt proud of themselves for making a difference in the little bird's life.

I AM BRAVE!

Noah and Millie were two courageous children who were always there for each other. They cheered for one another whenever they needed support.

One night, the two children went up to their room after having a long, tiring but fun day. Millie hopped into her bed and yawned as she placed her head on her pillow. Before getting into his bed, Noah turned on their night light which was near the window. It stayed on all night until the morning. Noah, like many children, liked having a soft light in the room at night.

A few minutes later, Mom and Dad came into the room to tuck them in. Noah and Millie each got a kiss from their parents. Then Mom and Dad said goodnight before turning off the main light and quietly leaving the room.

"Good night, Millie," Noah said sleepily.

"Good night, Noah," Millie said right back.

Noah smiled as he closed his eyes. A few minutes went by then Noah heard a soft click and everything went dark. The little boy's eyes grew wide as he sat up. It was so dark that he couldn't see anything! It was so quiet too.

All he could hear was the sound of his big sister breathing softly. She had a slight cold, so her breathing sounded almost like she was snoring.

But... What if it wasn't Millie? he thought to himself.

The little boy had a very colorful imagination. Whenever he played with his sister, he was able to imagine amazing adventures with her.

Now that he was sitting in the dark, Noah's vivid imagination came to life. As he listened to the soft snoring sound, he tried to imagine what it could be. It reminded him of his Grandma's coffee machine, but that couldn't be! She wasn't there, and there was no smell of fresh coffee. It couldn't be a wild animal, because the window was shut.

The little boy then noticed the sound of the clock ticking softly in the room.

But... What if it wasn't the clock? he thought to himself.

Noah imagined that maybe someone or something was tapping at their bedroom window, but who would do that at this time of night?

Noah was beginning to feel a little uneasy, but then he heard his sister's voice.

"What happened to the night light?" she asked.

Then Noah heard Millie's footsteps as she walked toward the window. Moments later, Noah heard the click of the night light switch, and the room was filled again with the soft glowing light he knew well.

"Noah? Why are you sitting up? And why are you still awake?" Millie asked.

"I... I woke up when the night light went out. And I kept hearing these strange sounds," he explained.

"Oh, right. You don't like the dark, do you?" Millie said as she walked over to her brother's bed.

She sat next to him and smiled, "I know that the sounds you hear when you're sitting in the darkness seem strange, and you imagine all sorts of things. But if you try to listen to those sounds, you might be able to find out where they're coming from. Let me show you."

Millie stood up once more and walked over to the light switch. She clicked it off, sat next to Noah again and asked, "Can you hear anything?"

"I can hear a ticking sound," Noah said. "It sounds like something tapping at the window."

"But that sound is only coming from the clock," Millie said in the darkness.

Millie was still sitting at her brother's side and said, "When you're trying to sleep, you should try to turn your imagination off. Then you will discover that there's nothing in the darkness to worry about. When you try to think about what is really causing the sounds you hear, you will soon realize that everything is fine," she said, as she gave Noah a squeeze.

Millie sat next to him in the darkness for a while longer, and very soon, Noah realized that his sister was right.

With Millie's help, Noah was able to fall asleep quickly. For the first time, he was able to sleep soundly, even without the night light.

What a brave little boy!

ONTO THE NEXT ADVENTURE...

Are you brave enough to face your fears just like Noah and Millie?

In these stories, Noah and Millie faced trials and bravely overcame obstacles, and even rescued a little trapped bird in distress.

Now, it's time for you to go on your own adventures and live your own unique stories. Don't be afraid to face life head-on and with the help of family and friends, you will surely be just as amazing as Noah and Millie.

Conclusion

I Hope You Enjoyed These Stories!

As we come to the end of our book, *Fun Bedtime Stories for Kids Ages 4-8*, we hope that the adventures of Noah and Millie have touched your hearts, sparked your imagination, and filled your nights with joy and wonder.

It has been our greatest pleasure to accompany you on this journey!

The bond between parent and child is strengthened through the shared experience of reading. As you reflect upon the stories and the lessons learned, may the wonder of these moments continue to resonate within your family.

The journey of childhood is a wondrous one, filled with growth, imagination, and endless possibilities. As you close this book, we encourage you to keep the spirit of adventure alive. Encourage your child to dream big, explore new horizons, and embrace the unique qualities that make them who they are.

"*Fun Bedtime Stories for Kids Ages 4-8*" is not just a book—it is a celebration of the love between a parent and child, the joy of discovery, and the power of storytelling. We hope it has kindled a lifelong love for reading in your little one, opening doors to new worlds, and inspiring their creative endeavors.

Thank you for allowing Noah and Millie to be a part of your family's bedtime routine.

As you embark on new adventures, remember that the greatest stories are the ones you create together—filled with love, laughter, and cherished memories.

With Gratitude and Warm Wishes,
Penelope Arnoll-Davis

YOUR BOOK REVIEW IS MORE THAN WORDS.

By sharing your thoughts about "*Fun Bedtime Stories For Kids Ages 4-8*" on Amazon, you can help other families find this collection of tales, ensuring that the fun and adventure continues to spread far and wide.

Thank you for choosing to be part of this story; the legacy of bedtime tales is kept alive by generous friends like you. You help us write the next chapter of dreams and adventures with each review.

Leaving a review on Amazon is easy and takes less than a minute. Simply scan the QR code below:

USA

For non-US residents choose from one of the QR codes below:

UK

ITALY

AUSTRALIA

CANADA

As we close this book and look forward to the next story, know that your support is deeply appreciated. Your book review will ensure that the wonder of our bedtime stories reaches every curious child's mind and fills them with contentment as they then happily drift off to sleep.

With heartfelt thanks,
Penelope Arnoll-Davis

Made in the USA
Las Vegas, NV
10 June 2024